MW00447024

WORDS
OF
POWER
AND
TRANSFORMATION

BY EMBROSEWYN TAZKUVEL

CELESTINE LIGHT MAGICK SERIES
ANGELS OF MIRACLES AND MANIFESTATION
144 Names, Sigils and Stewardships to Call the Magickal Angels of Celestine Light

WORDS OF POWER AND TRANSFORMATION
101+ Magickal Words and Sigils of Celestine Light to Manifest Your Desires

CELESTINE LIGHT MAGICKAL SIGILS OF HEAVEN & EARTH

SECRET EARTH SERIES
INCEPTION *(Book 1)*
DESTINY *(Book 2)*

PSYCHIC AWAKENING SERIES
CLAIRVOYANCE
TELEKINESIS
DREAMS

AURAS
How to See, Feel and Know

SOUL MATE AURAS
How Find Your Soul Mate & "Happily Ever After"

UNLEASH YOUR PSYCHIC POWERS

PSYCHIC SELF DEFENSE

LOVE YOURSELF
Secret Key To Transforming Your Life

22 STEPS TO THE LIGHT OF YOUR SOUL

ORACLES OF CELESTINE LIGHT
Complete Trilogy of Genesis, Nexus & Vivus

WORDS OF POWER

AND

TRANSFORMATION

101+ Magickal Words and Sigils of Celestine Light to Manifest Your Desires

EMBROSEWYN TAZKUVEL

Published by Kaleidoscope Productions
PO Box 3411; Ashland, OR 97520
www.kaleidoscope-publications.com
ISBN 978-0-938001-15-7

Illustrations, Layout and Design by Sumara Elan Love

Copyright 2016 by Embrosewyn Tazkuvel

All rights reserved
This book including the cover illustration, may not be copied except sigils for personal use by the original purchaser. The book may not be reproduced or retransmitted by any means in whole or part, or repackaged, resold, or given away for free as a download, in whole or part, in any form.

Distribution
Only legally available to be purchased as a paperback book through retail or online bookstores, or in eBook format through major online retailers and their affiliates.

PLEASE DO NOT PARTICIPATE IN PIRACY.

Disclaimer
Nothing in this book should be construed as medical advice.
If you have a health issue you should seek out a medical professional.

TABLE OF CONTENTS

Relationships and Interactions with Others

Develop Your Psychic Abilities

Health

INTRODUCTION

ven common words and phrases such as *stop!*, *I can*, *I can't*, *I hate you!*, *I love you*, can powerfully affect how we feel and how we act toward both ourselves and others. Simple subtle differences in words can also make a huge difference in effect.

Many university studies have proven the power of positive words and positive reinforcement to create superior results, while negative words and phrases produced negative affects in test subjects. There is literally magick in the common words we choose to speak; both magick to help and magick to hurt. Add in truly magickal words of Celestine Light that have dedicated and specific purposes of transformation, and what might have seemed impossible becomes possible and does so quickly.

My first exposure to the power of a single word was back in my idealistic church affiliated days when I was in my early twenties. It was about a month before I was scheduled to go on a mission for my church. I had the opportunity to have a private meeting with President Neff, the head of the mission in New York City where I lived at the time. Though I had been called to serve elsewhere, we were acquaintances and he asked me to visit him in his office on my last day in the city.

He was a little fellow, only a bit over five feet tall, but he was a feisty, spiritual giant. He spent a few minutes asking friendly questions about my family and wondering how much I was looking forward to my upcoming adventure. Then in a more serious tone he asked,

"Are you going to be the best missionary in your mission?"

I puffed up my chest a little and told him enthusiastically, "I am going to try my utmost to be the best missionary I can be."

13

I thought I had given a great answer. But President Neff obviously had a different opinion. "Stand up," he ordered me curtly. Without hesitation I quickly stood up in front of his desk. He stood up on the other side of it facing me.

"I didn't ask you if you were going to *try* to be the best missionary. I asked you if your were going to *be* the best missionary."

His reply was unexpected and I wasn't sure how to respond. It didn't seem to be in the spirit of humility to state that I would be the best. Nor did I even see how I could make that assumption as I did not know a single other person that was already serving there as a missionary. I tried to explain that to President Neff.

"Well you see, I know I will give it my best effort. You can count on that. But there are over one hundred young men and women serving in the mission I'm going to. I have never met even a single one of them. I don't think of missionary work as a competition. To state unequivocally that I will be the best is a fairly competitive way of looking at it. And even if I did look at it that way, how could I state I would be the best, when in essence I don't even know the efforts or capabilities of my competition?"

President Neff, short President Neff, reached across his desk, grabbed my shirt tightly in his fist and pulled me toward him so his face was very close to mine.

"If you are only going to *try* you will have no chance to achieve your potential. You will fail to achieve the excellence you could before you even begin." He released his hold on my shirt and motioned for me to sit back down as he sat in his own chair again.

"Thoughts are powerful," he elaborated, "spoken words even more so. If you state that you *will* be the best, if that is your firm focus and intent, what others do becomes irrelevant. Your statement of purpose will become the reality, as long as you retain your focus and intent."

Our meeting was soon over and I left president Neff's office shortly after his powerful pep talk, never to see or talk to him again. Though I didn't feel it at all in my mind or heart at that moment, before I said goodbye I looked him in the eye and told him, "President Neff, I *will* be the best missionary in my mission."

He smiled and nodded his head in appreciation. "Saying it aloud is the first step to making it reality." He gave me a friendly pat on the back as I walked out the door. "Now go out and *do it*!"

As the days passed I continued to reflect upon the mantra *'Be the best*

– *Do it!*' And to my own amazement, in my short time as a missionary, I did. The words propelled me, they inspired me and motivated me to achieve far more than I would ever have planned on doing before. And the difference was simply one word: "I will *be*" rather than "I will *try*."

Though this book is based upon using the magickal Words of Power and transformation revealed in Celestine Light, it is not necessary for you to even know what Celestine Light is for the words to be powerfully effective in your life. You can subscribe to any belief system, or none at all, and the Words of Power will still work their magick for you. Just as uttering special powerful words of the spoken language such as, *you're hired* or *you're fired*, or *I love you* and *will you marry me* can have immediate transformative affects.

Words of Power & Transformation is all about learning how to use specific words of uncommon power in precise ways, to help achieve your goals. Special magickal words and activating phrases have been revealed through Celestine Light that will stimulate dormant energies and latent powers within you, and coalesce potent energies from the world around you, to actualize that which you command with focus and intensity. *This book includes 101 transformational phrases containing 177 activating Words of Power and their accompanying Sigils* that will unlock many of the doors you wish to pass through when you use them in their harmony. But it is still up to you to followup with enough intent, focus and often times passion, to step into and embrace the potential of the portal you unlock.

SECTION I

Creating Personal Action Sigils

The Magick of I AM and I WILL

Relationship of Words of Power and Body Energy Centers

The Escalating Crescendo

WHERE DID THE MAGICKAL WORDS OF CELESTINE LIGHT COME FROM?

ecret magickal Words of Power have been used in prayers, hexes, curses, and incantations of manifestation and transformation by Shamans, Priests, Witches and Wizards, from the earliest recordings of written language. Ancient Egyptian and Greek papyri, such as the Graecae Magicae have been unearthed dating back as far as the 4th century BC that are full of magickal incantations.

Over time, involved rituals and incantations were often reduced down to their most powerful essence. Not unlike a modern writer who strives to convey the message of the story in the most concise and impactful way possible. For instance, in the first chapter of the Graecae Magicae, which goes into great ritualistic detail about how to acquire a supernatural assistant, a key part is reduced down to the Greek Words of Power "IAEOBAPHRENEMOUN" and "IARBATHA."

Celestine Light was founded by Yeshua of Nazareth over 2,000 years ago in the Holy Lands of the Middle East. Though modern Christians would be abhorred to consider that early Christians, including the apostles and highest leaders, employed spells and magickal powers, it was in fact quite common among Celestines. They viewed spells as concentrated forms of prayer and paranormal abilities as their birthright from God.

Not only were specific incantations, magickal tools and Words of Power introduced and taught by Yeshua, as recorded throughout the 800+ pages of the *Oracles of Celestine Light*, but his wife Miriam of Magdala, (better known in the modern world as Mary Magdalene) was held in awe and sometimes feared by all who knew her or had heard of her because of the unequaled magnitude of her magickal abilities.

Miriam's mastery of supernatural powers combined with her profound spirituality and many years as a personal witness to the teachings and majesty of Yeshua, culminated in her becoming the Angel of the Covenant. In addition to the Oracles, her deeply moving story is told in further detail in the books *Inception* and *Destiny*, as shared by her brother Lazarus of Bethany.

Though some come from other ancient sources, most of the Words of Power found within this book come from the teachings of Celestine Light. These are sacred words in the language of Elohim; the language of God. If we are endeavoring to use the most potent Words of Power, none could be greater than those used for the same purpose in the Celestine realms of Elohim.

There are two broad categories of Words of Power. The first, are used to create specific actions, such as physical or emotional healing, or to find a lost object or true love. The second, call in the assistance of specific angels of Elohim to help you achieve a purpose. Each angel has a particular stewardship and responsibility. Calling upon them with their activating word of power brings them to your assistance quicker than anything else you can do, including calling upon them by their name. This book will cover 101 of the most commonly desired purposes in the first category. The next book in the series will detail the Words of Power and the stewardships of all of the higher angels.

Some words you will see repeated in various phrases such as the words for *speed healing*, which are *Vastan Soolasee*. Repetition comes from the need to use the same words for different purposes, such as *speed healing from a physical injury* and *speed healing from a disease*.

Sometimes you can make the leap and assume that words repeated are equivalent words from the language of the Elohim into English; for instance *Vastan* being the equivalent of *speed*. However, there are other instances where one or two words may encompass an entire phrase, with no comparable word for word English equivalency such as *#84 Instantly Calm Your Anger*, which just translates into *Talialee*. In this and similar incidents, a single word captures the meaning of the entire phrase in English.

WHAT'S A SIGIL?

 sigil is a mark, symbol or sign that assists in calling forth the forces desired for magickal actions because it is the energetic resonance of the specific purpose. It is a symbolic representation of your desired outcome. In the case of angels or other unseen beings, the sigil is their personal resonance. Using a sigil often compels a response from angels and other supernatural beings. It also rapidly coalesces the energies of any purpose you are seeking to achieve.

Sigils have been used since before the written language existed. Some of the sigils used in Celestine Light, or parts of them, are of ancient origin, or stem from ancient cultures such as Egyptian and Mayan, or have various religious foundations such as Wicca, Paganism, early Christianity, Zoroastrianism, Hinduism or Kabbalahism. Sigils of angels preceded the emergence of magickal humans and have remained unchanged from the beginning of time.

The point of a sigil is to visually and aurically help you to attune to the resonance of the energy you are calling in. For instance, if you were trying to attract people with black hair but were holding up a sign of people with blonde hair, you probably would not be too successful. It is the same with many kinds of sigils. Some are specific and unchanging, such as the sigils of angels. Others created many hundreds of years ago, had significance at the time to the people who created them, but their energetic essence is lost on modern people.

Some of the sigils of Celestine Light incorporate imagery easier for modern people to relate to which facilitates an energetic connection to the magickal forces desired. For instance, if you are seeking knowledge, a sigil that incorporated the image of a book would more instantly attune you to the concept of knowledge than would an incomprehensible sigil designed by some wizard of bygone ages that to a modern viewer just appears as a series of random, meaningless lines.

Sigils and Words of Power will work separately and independent of the other. Putting the two together simply amplifies the energy and aids in your focus. Saying the word or Words of Power without a sigil will still effectively call in the energies you are seeking. Just looking at a sigil without saying any Words of Power will also call in the energy you seek. But combining them together will produce quicker and often more profound results.

Celestine Light symbols are designed to be most effective for a magickal incanter of this day and age. Some of them remain similar to the original design of their early creators because this has proven to be a vital, timeless pattern that continues to serve its energetic purpose well. Others are unique symbols of Celestine Light given by the Elohim and as such also remain unchanged. Many others blend recognizable modern images with potent unchanging magical images that retain and summon specific magickal energies, such as the pentagram, hexagram, five-sided star, six-sided star, crescent moon, sun, circles and arrows. Ultimately, whatever sigil is designated for a particular purpose, with whatever its unique shape may be, is the one that Adepts of Celestine Light have found to be the most effective, powerful and fast-acting.

WHY IS IT CALLED "MAGICK"

he word Magick, with variant spellings of Magik and Magique, seems to have originated in the 14th century in Europe. According to the English Wictionary, it derives from the Middle French magique, and several more ancient sources including, the Latin magica and magicus, and from ancient Greek magikos. Other influences on the word etymology include the Magi of Persia to whom the abilities of supernatural powers were often attributed. In the Middle English period of the 15th century the spelling was magike.

In literature, *magick* can be found as early as 1584 in writings of the Italian Giambattista della Porta. The *magick* variant was used more extensively in the 1600's, including the works of *Daphnis and Chloe* by Andrew Marvell, *Against Absence* by Sir John Suckling, and *Abraham Cowley* by Geoffrey Walton.

The spelling *magick* fell out of favor in the 18th and 19th century as stage magicians became more and more popular and used the spelling 'magic' for their acts of illusion.

In the early 20th century adding the *k* to the word magic became popularized once again by Aleister Crowley, a prominent occultist.

Why did the word ever have a *k*? Foremost, it obviously sounds the same as other spellings. It has also been theorized that the selection of *k* may have originally been influenced by numerology, which was very popular during the mid centuries. *K* is the 11th letter of the English alphabet. It represents illumination and is a very significant master number in numerology.

The element potassium may also have had an influence on spelling magick with a *k*. Alchemy was popular in the middle ages and potassium chloride was one of the most important chemicals used by conjurers and alchemists. It burns with a spellbinding red-pinkish-lavender-purple flame. Potassium is Kalium in Latin and is represented by the letter *K* on the Periodic Chart of Elements.

In *Celestine Light* we use Magick to consciously and purposefully influence ourselves, others, situations and events by calling in and harnessing unseen natural energies, spiritual forces and angelic powers.

Some of these supernatural manifestations and abilities lay dormant inside of us waiting to be unleashed. Using magick in the proper way makes your spirit soar and allows your true magnificent potential to come forth. We are all so much more than the frail bodies we inhabit.

By spelling Magick with a *k* we separate our mystical actions that produce very real and tangible results, from the transitory entertainment magic of stage magicians and illusionists.

Calling upon the forces available through Celestine Light Magick opens the doors to a vast array of paranormal powers and supernatural phenomena. Even a person that has never seen any evidence in themselves of paranormal abilities can quickly see some of those abilities pop up with a gusto by employing just a little Celestine Light Magick for a jump start.

The correct words, used in the proper manner, especially when accompanied by a resonating sigil, can produce some of the most immediate effective magick you can do and that is what this book will reveal to you.

MAGICKAL WORDS & SIGILS WORK
WITH ANY RELIGIOUS BELIEF

he rain falls and the sun shines on the crops of the farmer that is an atheist or agnostic as equally as it does for the farmer that believes fervently in God. Whether the believer is Jewish, Christian, Muslim, Hindu, Buddhist or any other religion, is equally irrelevant. If they are nearby neighbors, in the same geographic and climate location, they will all receive the same blessing of rain and sunshine for their crops.

The same principle of universal blessing applies to those who invoke the basic foundational Celestine Light Words of Power and sigils. Just like the words *I love you* immediately connect to your heart, these are words that connect to the divine, creative force of the universe regardless of who speaks them. They are keys that unlock and open doors of possibility and fulfillment, even for someone that may not believe there is anything behind the doors.

Consider an actual locked door. Perhaps in a strange, peculiar shaped building. You've been told to go to the 7th floor, then to the 7th hallway, then the 7th door and insert an intricate, antique golden key you have been given, into the door to unlock it. You've been promised that behind the door will be wonders to delight and amaze you. It all seems like nonsense, especially when you look at the key. It is very convoluted in shape and doesn't look like any key you have ever seen before. You seriously doubt whether it would open a door even if there happened to be a 7th door in the 7th hallway on the 7th floor.

When you arrive at the building you discover to your displeasure that there are no elevators, no instant way up to the 7th floor. Grumbling to yourself, you reluctantly climb 7 flight of stairs, mumbling more with the exertion of each flight about the waste of time. Finally arriving out of breath on the 7th floor you count the hallways that diverge off as you pass them until you arrive at the 7th that veers off to the right. Now counting doors, you are relieved to discover that at least there really is a 7th door and it does have a peculiar keyhole.

Still doubting, but at least giving a little credence to the possibility that the key might fit in the door, you insert it into the keyhole and slowly turn the door knob. The door swings open suddenly and so do your eyes in amazement, both that the key actually worked and at the unfathomable wonders the open door has revealed.

Magickal Words of Power and Sigils are like the mysterious key that opened the 7th door down the 7th hall on the 7th floor. Insert the correct key into the keyhole and no matter how disbelieving a person might be the key will still work to open the door. Or in this case, the Word of Power and sigil will work to call in the energy to which it has a resonance.

That said, the results will often be amplified and occur more rapidly in proportion to ones faith and belief in the divine or even in just the action you are taking. The particulars of ones faith are of little importance when using *Words of Power* that affect everyday life: Pagan, Catholic, Wicca, Protestant, Jewish, Occultist, Muslim, New Age, Buddhist, Hindu or even the popular undefined *spiritual*. Just believing in something, some energetic force, some power greater than what men or women could manifest on their own, aids in calling those unseen energies to you for your benefit. This is because faith itself, in all of its diverse forms, is the greatest power in the universe. And anything faith is applied to happens quicker and with greater potency and fulness.

Just as any subject at school is learned through increasing levels of complexity and depth, Celestine Light Magick runs from simple but effective basic magick to more complex and very, very potent reality altering transformations. Advanced Celestine Light magick can only be invoked by experienced practitioners; some only by Adepts.

This book includes many of the most useful and commonly needed transformational words and phrases, plus some of the more advanced ones. The criteria for inclusion of the 89 phrases and sigils in Section II were power words and sigils that would be useful and work for anyone regardless of their religious beliefs or lack thereof, have a noticeable effect, be easily invoked, quickly effectively.

The initiating energy is in the words and sigils, which invoke forces that are universal in nature. Just as the sun shines and the rain falls on every person, good or bad, regardless of their beliefs, so too will those words and sigils work for anyone without any additional action required. Belief in a divine force greater than oneself will amplify the results, sometimes dramatically. But lack of such a belief will not prevent results from occurring.

The 12 Words of Power and sigils found in Section III are of a more advanced nature. This section is intended merely to introduce you to some of the higher level Celestine Light Words of Power and sigils. There are additional actions that must be taken to highly activate the magickal energies called to coalesce by these words and sigils. The foundation of those additional required actions is beyond the scope of this book and in most cases requires direct personal instruction by a Celestine Light Adept. Anyone interested in pursuing higher level magick is welcome to contact me through my website: *www.embrosewyn.com*.

CAVEATS

here are a few caveats:
  *Your need has to be real and genuine.
  *Whatever you are seeking to accomplish, it cannot harm any other person directly or indirectly, unless you are using power words in defense of your own well being from physical, emotional, mental or psychic attacks from another person.

*You also should not use Celestine Light magick to gain advantage for yourself at the disadvantage of someone else. For instance, you can use #85 Excel in a Competition, to coalesce dynamic energies to help you succeed far beyond your normal abilities in any type of competition. But you cannot use it to cause your opponent to do worse than they would normally do.

*Using Celestine Light magickal Words of Power is not a game and never should be treated as such if you actually want to get results. Speaking and invoking the magickal Words of Power coalesces potent divine energies around you and is literally transformative. Make sure you truly want and need that which the magickal words call upon before you invoke them. The sincerity and soberness of your efforts does make a difference.

* You do not need to believe in magick, divine power, angels or universal energies to derive benefit from using Celestine Light Words of Power. But belief in all of those, or at the very least a divine, benign higher force in some form, will amplify the affects because it helps you to connect in your heart, mind and psychic centers to the higher resonance energies you are calling upon. Keep an open mind as to the possibilities and you should see excellent results. If you absolutely doubt the validity of the *Words of*

Power, magick, or any form of higher divine energy, you would be best not to begin. No matter what endeavor in life you choose, from using Celestine Light magickal Words of Power, to proposing to the girl of your dreams, to running a race or starting a business, if you completely doubt your possibility of success you will get what you expect- failure. The more you are invested mentally and emotionally in a positive outcome the more you draw the energies to you to succeed.

*Celestine Light magickal words and sigils also tend to produce long lasting results. Because of that, it is important that you are truly prepared and ready for the change you desire.

WHY MAGICKAL WORDS & SIGILS
QUICKLY PRODUCE RESULTS

he magickal Words and Sigils of Celestine Light are specific activating words and symbols of angels and free flowing universal energies that can be used with equal effect by both complete novices or spell casting Adepts.

Like the blessings of angels, the free flowing universal energies remain unperceived and unknown to most people. But they are ever present valuable aids in your life when you become aware of them and their uses. They are as prevalent as every breath of air we breathe and can be very helpful when you understand how to separate them from the chaos of surrounding energies and focus them on the purpose best suited for their energy.

Whether you are devoutly religious and have used the power of prayer to affect changes, or are a beginner or advanced spell caster, enchanter or enchantress, you will find great value in the *Celestine Light Words of Power and transformation.* Add them to your prayer, spell or enchantment and watch the miracles and magick really begin!

As an Adept of Celestine Light, strongly connected to the divine source, I have used advanced Celestine Light magick for decades with amazing life saving and changing results for both myself and others. Yet, even with the great secrets I know, I most often still employ basic Celestine Light Words of Power and sigils when I call in forces beyond my own psychic and paranormal abilities, because they are so quickly and specifically effective.

How quick? In many cases, especially if it involves a change in, or effect upon you personally, the transformation begins from the moment you speak the Celestine Light Words of Power or even just look with focused intent at a sigil. If you seek tangible results in real life, manifestation of your desires may be as close as just a few spoken words or a momentary intense glance.

Many purposes that you might use the words of power and sigils for lend themselves to rapid manifestation, often times after just a single utterance of the Words of Power and/or an intense focused glance at the sigil. Others require more time looking at the sigil and saying the Words of Power multiple times during the day. For instance, you may invoke #27 *Attract True Love /Soul Mate*. While speaking the Words of Power and looking at the sigil one time may call your Soul Mate to ring your doorbell a few minutes later, the more likely reality is your true love may not even live in the same town Z you. It may take days, weeks and even months for the simple logistics of the two of you being in the same place at the same time to occur. When your objective is one that does not lend itself to instant or very rapid results, you should continue to say the Words of Power and look at the sigil every day. Two or three times a day is fine, or more often as well. Every time you speak the words or look at the sigil you are calling in the energy of manifestation and amplifying its power by your continued focus and repetition.

More complex spells and enchantments are very useful in harnessing specific universal energies to help fulfill our desires. But often times a similar effect can be obtained simply by gazing with focus on a connecting sigil or uttering the appropriate Celestine Light magickal word or short phrase of power, without using ritual, rhyme or anything complex, nothing more than your simple spoken words; when they are the right words.

If you are in a dangerous situation, or a public place with an immediate need, you can whisper the Celestine Light magickal Words of Power, or even think them in your head to gain an immediate advantage. Common sense and awareness of your surroundings and risky situations can also be a great assist in keeping you safe.

Though the Celestine Light Words of Power are very effective, I am not implying that they take the place of more advanced and complex prayers or spiritual/magickal rituals. While Words of Power and sigils can be used alone with marvelous affect, they can also be combined with additional prayers or magickal rituals, spells or enchantments for even greater results.

Most people are surprised and even amazed at how quickly Celestine Light sigils and/or Words of Power can manifest their desired intent for most objectives.

A perfect example of how quickly results can occur happened while I was writing this book. We have a little Honda Elite motorcycle. A couple of weeks previously, I had lost the sole ignition key on the very day before I was going to take it to the locksmith to make a duplicate key. Both my wife and I looked everywhere for that key, which was on a tagged keyring. We searched in every pocket of every pair of pants, in every drawer, in every part of the car, every place in the Jeep and on every table, shelf and counter in the house. We both searched multiple times, covering every possibility at least twice.

I contacted the dealer and they said they had no way to provide a duplicate. Next, I called a locksmith. He said he could come up to the house and make a duplicate that might work for $150.

During this time my wife Sumara had been working on creating digital images of the 101+ sigils for this book. She and I had to go to an appointment and as I passed through the office to get her, she was just finishing up thirty minutes of work on the sigil for finding a lost or hidden object. She pointed to the image on her computer screen. "I want you to look at that honey. We need to find that key. I don't want to have to pay $150 for something we already have."

I took a quick glance at the sigil, nodded my head in agreement and then we had to hurry out the door to not be late for our meeting. When we got in the Jeep the first thing Sumara did was to open the glove compartment. I knew it was going to be a fruitless effort as both of us had already looked in that little cubby hole multiple times and had come up empty.

However, anyone who has ever misplaced something remembers how even though you know better, you continue to relook in places you have already looked, just hoping that somehow this time would produce different results. And lo and behold to both of our astonishment, this time it did! Immediately after opening the glove compartment door Sumara reached in and pulled out the key leaning against the left interior wall!

How had we both missed it before? I didn't know the answer to that question. But I did know we had just seen another undeniable manifestation of how quickly sigils can work. Sumara had been extremely focused on that sigil as she created it digitally for the half hour just before finding the key. Her focus called in its energy. And she got nearly instant results just from using a sigil! So you can imagine the magick that can happen when you combine sigils with Words of Power!

USING CELESTINE LIGHT
MAGICK IS SAFE

ue to misleading themes in movies and books, novices are often worried that using magickal words will put them at risk of either being drawn into darker magick or even as Karmic punishment for using magick to create an unfair advantage. This should not even be the slightest worry when you are invoking Celestine Light Words of Power.

If you are using a word or phrase that calls upon the stewardship of an angel, they will only oblige your invocation if your intent is of the light.

The same holds true when you use the Celestine Light magickal words revealed in this book to call in transformational universal energies. Each magickal word or phrase constructed from the words has been carefully selected by Adepts of the Celestine Light from the hundreds of Words of Power available, to help you achieve your desires and goals by utilizing the energy of light, not darkness.

That's not to say that there are not instances when using magick does come back to bite someone. When people get into more advanced magick, they very likely will have unpleasant complications if they start invoking unjustified curses or other magick that is harmful to others. But magick that is purely of the light, which is the only kind found within this book, is safe and beneficial to you and others of good intent – always!

USING CELESTINE LIGHT
MAGICK IS FAIR

 ome people worry that using magickal words to help achieve their goals and desires is unfair. The reality is that knowledge is power and it is power fairly earned by applying the effort to seek out the knowledge and acquire it. The knowledge of *Celestine Light magickal Words of Power* found within these pages are readily available to anyone that purchases the book. If they choose not to do so, or have no interest in such powers, that is their choice. It in no way makes it unfair for you to choose the opposite and be able to employ magickal Words of Power and sigils for your benefit.

The situation is no different than an athlete who does well in their event because they chose to put in the time and effort to perfect their techniques, while the losing athletes may have chosen not to make the same commitment. In my youth I wrestled and participated in karate and judo competitively. If I took the time to learn how to execute a new hold or throw and defeated my opponent with it, was it unfair that I used a technique they did not know or had not mastered? Of course not, and it is just as fair to learn and use Celestine Light Magick to your advantage.

ADDING SIGILS

nlike vivid imagery which may differ from person to person in preference, sigils are special images that serve very specific purposes and summonings. Many Celestine Light magickal endeavors have sigils that can be used to facilitate their purpose. Some are ancient and connect to specific angels and other unseen beings and those may be fairly cryptic to modern people. Others are more recognizable, with visual components that are designed to help you more quickly and thoroughly connect to the energies that will serve your purpose.

Each Celestine Light magickal word of power has an accompanying sigil. If you are looking at the sigil as you speak the magickal word aloud, the effect, intensity and rapidity of the magickal energy will be enhanced.

COMBINE MAGICKAL WORDS WITH COMMON WORDS OF ANY LANGUAGE

he magickal Words of Power revealed in this book can be used alone or in conjunction with any number of supporting words in any language. Intent is a very important aspect of success using Magick. Using common words in addition to the magickal words can amplify the effects of the magickal words, provided the common words chosen are in harmony and focus with the magickal words.

For instance, perhaps you desire to get rid of a bad habit but are constantly finding you simply do not have enough will power to resist all the temptations. You could just speak aloud the Celestine Magickal words *Ra Q Lon Baronde*, any time you are tempted. Uttering *Ra Q Lon Baronde* aloud will instantly increase your will power and steel your resolve. Adding the special magickal/common words *I AM* with an appropriate very common word such as *strong*, will increase the power of the magick. Temptation is now thwarted by *Ra Q Lon Baronde! I AM Strong!*

Nor should you underestimate or disregard the innate magickal power of common words to strengthen and coalesce the energies you desire. If the intent of the words, in any language, concisely convey the desired outcome they have more power to help create the outcome than words that are not as vividly descriptive when they are added to appropriate dedicated magickal words of Celestine Light. Here are some examples added to the magickal words *Zonta Varbon*, a magickal combination used to amplify your auric energy for powerful actions.

Zonta Varbon! I focus energy explosively!

Zonta Varbon! I create change suddenly!
Zonta Varbon! I transform the ordinary into the extraordinary!
Zonta Varbon! I AM impishly playful!
Zonta Varbon! I exude passion!

Please note in the above examples how everything is stated as existing fact and not as hoped for goals. Not *I will focus energy explosively*, but fait accompli, *I focus energy explosively!*

COMBINE MAGICKAL WORDS AND SIGILS WITH POWERFUL IMAGERY

 f you are not looking for an instant fix, but are on a multi-day or longer path of change, you should consider adding relevant, powerful imagery to your use of Celestine Light magickal Words of Power and sigils. For instance, perhaps you desire to lose weight. In addition to the sigil that accompanies the Word of Power for losing weight, another potent image would be to find a picture of a person that has the body you desire to have, then replace their head with yours, so their body now becomes your body in the picture.

Imagery is equally effective with instant or short term transformations, but is more often employed in changes that will take some days to evolve.

COMBINE MULTIPLE MAGICKAL WORDS
FOR ADDED BENEFIT

n addition to adding images to see and common words to the magickal invocations you say, you can also combine as many Celestine Light magickal words as you feel appropriate to reinforce and empower the magickal utterance or incantation. For instance, using the losing weight example again, a person with that stated objective might want to combine the magickal words and purposes that activate and empower: #46 create a desire to eat healthier + #14 eliminate desires for harmful habits + #54 motivation to exercise + #56 increase metabolism to lose weight.

HOW TO ACTIVATE THE MAGICKAL WORDS OF POWER IN YOUR LIFE

t would be nice if all you needed to do was to casually speak a Celestine Light magickal Word of Power and presto, your grand desire was immediately manifested. We would all be millionaires, with wonderful jobs, fantastic health and perfect, fulfilling relationships if that were the case. While there are many desired outcomes that lend themselves to rapid and even instant results such as #81 Invoke a Circle of Protection Against Psychic Attacks, some take longer simply by the logistics of their nature.

Additionally, anything worthwhile does require some level of passion and focus to activate the path to success. It is the same with the magickal words. The more focus and intensity of desire that you bring to the issue, coupled with optimum use of magickal words and sigils, the greater the power you call forth to come to you, and the more startling your results can be. Add in at least a modicum of faith and persistence and you have all the magickal ingredients for success. Add in greater faith + a passionate desire to manifest the outcome + persistent focus and you whip up a recipe for great success!

Be Interested In The Outcome

Your first step, regardless of what magickal objective you are trying to achieve, is to be interested enough in the outcome that you can engender a passionate desire for the result in your heart and a clarity of focus in your mind that will not be distracted by other thoughts or feelings when you are invoking the magical words and actively seeking your objective. This is a critical first step. Nothing further should be ventured until these essential tools are a part of your being in regards to the magickal outcome you seek.

Number Of Times To Repeat The Words Of Power

There is not a prescribed or ritualistic number of times you need to repeat the Words of Power or look at the sigil. However, as they are laid out on the sigil page, the Words of Power should be spoken aloud a minimum of three times successively with increasing power in your voice each time. Though you are speaking the words three times, it is considered as one invocation. For some people with a burning passion to manifest their desire, once will be enough, when it is logistically possible for that to occur. But for most, more is better as the frequency helps to maintain your focus on your goal and desire.

Some purposes for which you are using Celestine Light magick, such as #84 *Calm Anger in Yourself or Others*, are ones that the magick will work almost instantly as long as you have an adequate focus and desire. Other objectives such as #78 *Start a Successful Business From Your Passion*, by their nature will take longer to manifest. For those objectives that by their nature will take a little time to occur, looking at the sigil regularly and speaking the Words of Power daily or more often continues to call in the energy and amplify and speed up its effects.

Focus On One Objective At A Time

To magnify your focus, you should only be endeavoring to achieve a single objective at a time. Often this will mean only using a single sigil and the accompanying words of power until your goal is achieved. However, you may use multiple sigils and words of power to good effect if they are all directly related to your objective. For instance, #69 *Have Money Come To You Unexpectedly* and #70 *Increase Your Income*, have a good synergy together. Using them in tandem can amplify the results from both objectives.

Memorization Of The Words And Sigil Is Helpful

The main thrust still still needs to be maintaining a focus on your goal and an intensity of your desire. Personally, I will memorize the words of power for my objective, such as #22 *Attract People Into Your Life That Can*

Help You. The words of power for #22 are "*jataash wiseef.*" I will memorize the words and repeat them frequently throughout the day. When I am alone I will say them aloud forcefully. When I am around others I will whisper them softly under my breath. In conjunction, I will memorize the image of the sigil so I can close my eyes and easily picture it in my mind. These two techniques firmly maintain and amplify my focus on the purpose. Stir in a passion to see the outcome manifest and you have the perfect magickal recipe for success!

FOLLOWUP ACTIONS TO AMPLIFY YOUR SUCCESS

t is not at all uncommon to see quick and sometimes immediate effects from using Celestine Light magickal words and sigils. Especially when you add in some of the other elements previously mentioned, such as harmonious common words and vivid imagery. Yet, even more potency, with quicker and greater success, can be achieved by supportive followup actions.

For instance, returning again to the losing weight theme, after speaking the magickal words, and viewing the images, you are likely to have a strong urge to begin exercising, even if it is only small steps to begin. A followup action to support the urge would be to join the YMCA or a gym. This puts you in an environment that further supports and encourages you to exercise and also has professional trainers to help insure you do so safely and optimally for your age and weight.

Or perhaps you are seeking true love. You have spoken the magick words and opened the door, but your true love has not yet come knocking. It may have something to do with seldom leaving the house or interacting with new people. A supportive action would be to join clubs, social causes, interest groups or any other opportunity that would put you among new, quality people with similar interests. The more opportunity you give the magick to happen, the more likely it is to occur.

THE POWER OF THE NUMBERS
3, 6, 9 & 12

n all of magick, not just magickal words, the power and effect of whatever you are doing is amplified significantly by repeating it three times, preferably aloud. Whether it is one word, a phrase or several sentences of an enchantment, it should be repeated three times aloud, one right after the other, with greater vocal force and passion each time. Oftentimes, speaking aloud the magickal words, phrase or enchantment three times is actually necessary to manifest the purpose. It's as if the angels or universal forces you are calling upon want to make sure you are serious by the evidence of three repetitive incantations before the forces are unleashed to come to your aid.

Repeating the word, phrase or enchantment three times is usually sufficient for most purposes. But if you truly feel extra emphasis would be helpful you can repeat it three times three. The nine repetitions should all be done one after the other rather than spread out nine times during the day or night. This is easier when you are only repeating one or a few words, but can become cumbersome if you have a lengthy involved incantation.

All the first three multiples of the number three exert special influences and energy on most circumstances. These include 3x2=6, 3x3=9 and 3x4=12. In Celestine Light many magickal group actions take place using these numbers. For instance 3 is the minimum number for a Qrom, a group of similar magickal ability to form a Circle of Power to create a magickal action or to make a decision or choice that will affect the entire group.

Likewise, when a Circle of Power is formed to create big magickal changes, six people in the circle is actually a more harmonious and conducive union than seven or eight people in the circle. So too is nine in a Circle of Power, a better number of participants than ten or eleven.

The ultimate number of participants for creating Circles of Power is twelve. Beyond that the circle will only gain marginal strength by adding more people and in many cases may actually have less strength. In order for Circles of Power to be as fully effective as possible, everyone in the circle must be very focused on its purpose and of one heart and one mind, while the circle is actively creating the magick. This has been proven to be challenging when the circle contains thirteen or more people. Just too many individual lives, with individual thoughts, emotions and circumstances they may be dealing with that day, to easily attain the perfect group synergy needed during the activation of the Circle of Power.

CREATING PERSONAL ACTION SIGILS

lthough each of the 101 topics included in this book come with an associated sigil, you can also create customize sigils for purposes unique to you, to add even greater power to your use of magickal words. The very fact that you are creating the sigil will give it more influence than a standard sigil because your energy is greatly imbued in it as you conceive and create it. As you are creating it to assist you in a specific and personal purpose, you are concentrating the energy of focused intent and that is powerful magick!

Here's how you do it:

1. Make a statement of what it is you intend to gain. For this example let's say, *I will find true love*.

2. Write the statement removing all vowels except the first *I*. That becomes Iwllfndtrlv.

3. Take that and remove any duplicate letters, leaving just one. That becomes Iwlfndtrv.

4. Reduce the number of letters to 9 or less, with 7 being the ideal number, as statistically in a roll of two dice, it is most likely to come up of all the numbers, giving your sigil the most likely energy to occur. In this case, the remaining letters are the same as they already equaled seven: Iwlfndtrv.

5. Rearrange the remaining letters in a stacked, creative manner inside a circle or shape of your choice.

6. Artistically enhance the letter stacking to create a custom, personal sigil for your stated purpose.

7. You can also insert images in place of letters as part of your artistic

sigil creation. For instance, a picture of an eye could take the place of the letter 'I.' This is very appropriate for anything having to do with finding something, as there is a dual meaning with the eye symbol representing you and the letter *I* as well as representing searching and looking for something.

THE MAGICK OF I AM AND I WILL

n any language *I AM* and *I WILL* are two of the most potent and fast acting words you can say to coalesce energy inside and out to achieve your desires. Because they are common frequently used words in every language, they are seldom recognized as magickal words. But if the purpose of employing magickal words is to initiate rapid

beneficial changes, then I AM and I WILL are two of the most effective combinations you will ever find to affect tangible, lasting change. Best of all, they work in any language!

Of course the words that proceed or follow are also vitally important. For example, in the Introduction I told the story of meeting President Neff. In that instance, I used the magickal words *I WILL*. But the first time I followed it with *try*, which is a word that drained all the magickal power out of I WILL. After President Neff educated me, I replaced *try* with *be*, a strongly positive word that supported the magick of I WILL. Instead of the limp energy of *I will try*, I called up the empowered energy of I WILL BE.

I WILL can produce instant results even for everyday actions. For instance, today I had to go to the local co-op during the peak lunch hour.

This store is notorious for extremely limited parking. Even during the slack times of the day it is difficult to find a parking space and may frustratingly require circling the block three to four times before you have success.

I make a habit of simply avoiding the store during the busy times of the day. But today I couldn't avoid it. I didn't want to have to get locked into the congestion of the small main parking lot, so as I was approaching the turn for the road that ran next to the store, a road that only has a few parking spaces which are always occupied, I said aloud, *I WILL find a parking space on this road*. Within seconds after turning the corner I saw a car pulling out from the space that literally was the closest location you could park to the store.

There is always a continual stream of cars on the road. One had turned shortly before me and two others were turning behind me. If I had not turned at that exact moment I would not have been the car in line to get the parking space just as a car was pulling out. Coincidence? I think not.

I AM is an equally powerful magickal word statement. Try it with just your name to feel the instant power course through you. Say, *I AM (your name)*, and fill your name into the blank. Say it three times and emphasize your name the most. Feel the power?

When you speak aloud and with force I AM (your name) it immediately activates and expands all of your energy centers, particularly your Qo, the center of self-confidence.

If you are ever in a situation where you doubt your ability to succeed, simply say *I AM (your name)*. This will instantly pump you full of self-confidence, and greatly increase the likelihood of success at your endeavor. If you know your Soul Name you can use it in place of your given name for an even more powerful result.

I AM is such a potent magickal combination of words that it is even mentioned in direct association with the identity of God in the Torah and Old Testament. In Exodus 3:13-14, "*Moses said to God, Behold, when I come to the children of Israel, and shall say to them, The God of your fathers has sent me to you; and they shall say to me, What is his name? what shall I say to them? And God said to Moses, I AM THAT I AM: and he said, Thus shall you say to the children of Israel, I AM has sent me to you.*"

It is not merely your name that gives you empowered benefits from association with I AM. Literally any positive word you put after I AM expands the power of that word within you. For instance, *I AM happy, I AM excited, I AM brilliant, I AM a success, I AM rich, I AM lucky.*

But the magick works both ways and the word or words that follow I AM are just as important as the two initiating words. Just as positive words bring about positive results, negative following words will produce an unfavorable result. Words such as: *I AM sad, I AM tired, I AM stupid, I AM an idiot, I AM a failure, I AM broke, I AM unlucky.*

The energy in these positive or negative following words is so potent and the affects so immediate that it is palpable. Even reading the words you can feel the affect both good and bad, inside of you, regardless of how you previously felt just seconds before. If you say them aloud, even if you do not at that moment feel that way, you will feel the influencing energy, either positive or negative, stir inside of you.

One of the really helpful aspects of the magickal words I AM is the ability to use them to almost instantly change a negative mood to a positive one. Perhaps you truly are a bit sad because of events that have occurred in your life that day or recently. That sadness may linger for an entire day or longer unless you take action to do something about it. Here's what to say: *I AM (your name)*, followed by *I AM happy.*

Even if you are so far from being happy that it is difficult to even say the word, saying these two phrases coupled with a little visualization will begin to lighten your mood quickly. Soon sadness will be replaced with happiness or whatever other positive mood you decided you wanted to have.

For visualization, picture one of the big old sailing ship wheels, the ones with many handles sticking out around the perimeter. See that wheel right in front of your body. It is connected to your heart and controls your emotions. Whatever handle is sticking out at the top of the wheel is your current emotion. Each of the other handles represent different emotions.

If sadness is your current emotional state, that is the handle protruding up from the top of the big circular wheel. It's opposite, happiness, will be the handle located 180 degrees away, down at the bottom of the wheel. As you say the magical phrases aloud, preferably three times in a row, visualize turning the wheel, moving sadness away from the top and moving happiness up to the top position. You will be amazed at how quickly the transformation in your emotional state occurs!

XE   Violet

KA   Dark Blue

QO   Blue Green

JA   Green

ZA   Yellow

WZ   Orange Yellow

VM   Red

RELATIONSHIP OF WORDS OF POWER
AND BODY ENERGY CENTERS

ost people have heard of the Chakra system of identifying the location of specific types of energy centers in the body. In Celestine Light we use a similar but more detailed system called the *Root Ki's* (keys) that is more useful because of the greater emphasis on the relationships between energy centers and the subtitles of the auric field.

Many of the magickal Words of Power directly affect one of the energy centers of the body or another. Hence, you will find the words for the Root Kis – Xe, Ka, Qo, Ja, Za, Wz and Vm part of many of the power words.

The names of the Root Kis are themselves magickal words of power. Here is what Yeshua said in the ***Oracles of Celestine Light: Vivus chapter 51*** as he introduced the Root Kis to his followers when he taught them the power of the **Lanaka:**

11 I am going to explain to you now about the seven abodes of aeon in your body and the eighth that is formed when all seven are in health and harmony with one another.

12 The name for each one was not chosen at random, but is an essential name, for the sound of it spoken embodies the essence of the aeon and induces it to become more active within you.

13 Merely speaking the name of the aeon attunes your spirit and body to that abode of power.

14 Some of the sounds may not be familiar to you because of your native tongue. Therefore, let all learn together some of the melodies of Heaven.

15 *Your seven personal aeons of power, including the eighth when it is formed, are called the Lanaka.*

16 *The sacred sounds of your aeons of power, beginning at the top and following to the bottom, are Xe (zēē), Ka (käh), Qo (kwōh), Ja (jäh), Za (zāy), Wz (wĭz), and Vm (vĭm).*

17 *The aeons of power align vertically, and there is a powerful relationship between all of them, as well as groups of them.*

18 *When all of these are in harmony and unison, they create an eighth aeon of power, the sound of Oo (oo), which appears not in one place, but everywhere in you and outside of you. Your aeon of Oo radiates from the core of your soul. It fills you and everyone and everything around you that it reaches with the essence of your desire.*

19 *Understanding the Lanaka within you is essential to your ability to channel the aeons of Heaven. It is not enough to merely learn of these seats of power and how to enliven them. You must also learn how they relate one to another and how to attune and harmonize groups together for specific purposes.*

THE ESCALATING CRESCENDO

hen you speak aloud the Celestine Light magickal Words of Power, you should be looking intently at the corresponding sigil or sigils if you are combining power words and sigils for a custom purpose. To achieve maximum and most rapid results, you should repeat the *Words of Power* three times and each time say them with greater force and conviction.

For example, if you were activating the power word and Sigil #76, to *Obtain Your Ideal Employment*, you would see the sigil at the top and the Words of Power in three upward steps of increasing size from smallest on the bottom, to largest on the top nearest the sigil. Use the increasing size to remember to say the word louder and with more force and desire as you repeat it from lowest to highest. End with your eyes steadily focused upon the sigil.

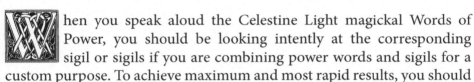

SUDAS BORLATAY VICAN

SUDAS BORLATAY VICAN

SUDAS BORLATAY VICAN

SECTION II

Change and Improve Yourself

Relationships and Interactions with Others

Develop Your Psychic Abilities

Health

Money & Success

Career & School

CELESTINE LIGHT MAGICKAL
WORDS & SIGILS

 hese are not ancient Hebrew, Hindu, Egyptian, Chinese, Persian, Greek or other symbols from long ago. Those images certainly had meaning to the people thousands of years ago that began using them as aids to bring in magickal energy. With the exception of personal sigils of angels and other unseen beings, ancient sigils would be meaningless and referenceless to you today.

For magick to work optimally, the energy of what you are seeking to accomplish has to flow inside of you. Everything you do to invoke the magick, from the words you say, the rituals you conduct, and the symbols and images you utilize, should have a direct connection from your heart, mind and psychic energy centers to what you are trying to accomplish.

In a simplistic example, if you were endeavoring to become a better fisherman and were using magick to amplify your success, which image below would you most quickly resonate with for that purpose?

The sigils that follow were carefully crafted and tested by Adepts of Celestine Light to retain the connections to ancient energies while resonating deeply with modern summoners of the magick power.

CHANGE AND IMPROVE YOURSELF

BECOME MORE LOVING AND LOVEABLE

JAMOVASAN
JAMOVASAN
JAMOVASAN

jah-mo-vah-sahn

Pronunciation File #1

BECOME MORE PASSIONATE

JAAZ VAASHTATAN
JAAZ VAASHTATAN
JAAZ VAASHTATAN

jahz vaash-ta-tahn

Pronunciation File #2

BECOME MORE SELF-CONFIDENT & EMPOWERED

QOBAKON
QOBAKON
QOBAKON

qwhoh-bah-kon

Pronunciation File #3

BECOME MORE BALANCED

ZINGGNIZ
ZINGGNIZ
ZINGGNIZ

zing-guh-nihz

Pronunciation File #4

BECOME LESS CRITICAL

HOOVAUSH
HOOVAUSH
HOOVAUSH

who-vawsh

Pronunciation File #5

BECOME MORE DISCERNING

ZDELANDA
ZDELANDA
ZDELANDA

zee-deh-lahn-dah

Pronunciation File #6

GAIN MORE SELF RESPECT

QOVOOKA
QOVOOKA
QOVOOKA

qwhoh-voo-kah

Pronunciation File #7

BECOME MORE SPONTANEOUS & PLAYFUL

JEETEEWEE
JEETEEWEE
JEETEEWEE

gee-tee-wee

Pronunciation File #8

INCREASE YOUR LUCK

ISHSHATAR
ISHSHATAR
ISHSHATAR

ish-shah-tar

Pronunciation File #9

RELEASE USELESS GUILT
OR SHAME

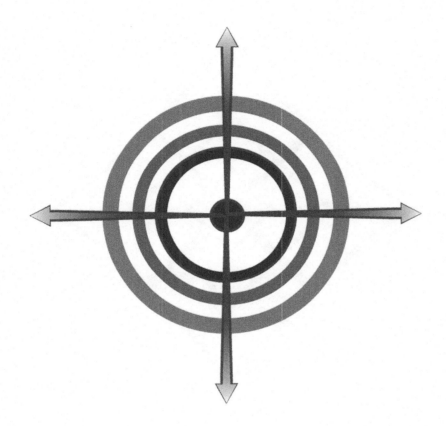

GAUSSA SABO
GAUSSA SABO
GAUSSA SABO

gaws-sah sah-bow

Pronunciation File #10

INCREASE YOUR ABILITY TO FOCUS ON A TASK

KAZEEZ VONTOUR
KAZEEZ VONTOUR
KAZEEZ VONTOUR

kah-zeez vohn-tour

Pronunciation File #11

INCREASE YOUR SPIRITUALITY & CLOSENESS TO THE DIVINE

ELOHIM JAKAXE
ELOHIM JAKAXE
ELOHIM JAKAXE

el-oh-heem jah kah zee

Pronunciation File #12

TURN YOUR WEAKNESS INTO YOUR STRENGTH

ZOICE EXTOOZAR
ZOICE EXTOOZAR
ZOICE EXTOOZAR

zoyce ex-too-zar

Pronunciation File #13

HAVE THE WILLPOWER TO RESIST TEMPTATION AND OVERCOME BAD HABITS

RA Q LON BARONDE
RA Q LON BARONDE
RA Q LON BARONDE

rah cue lohn bah-ron-day

Pronunciation File #14

BE MOTIVATED TO STOP PROCRASTINATING

ZEEATAR YAB
ZEEATAR YAB
ZEEATAR YAB

zee-ahtar yahb

Pronunciation File #15

OVERCOME ADDICTION

ZEEATAR KANONDUH
ZEEATAR KANONDUH
ZEEATAR KANONDUH

zee-ah-tar kah-nohn-duh

Pronunciation File #16

DISCOVER YOUR PURPOSE IN LIFE WITH A CLEAR VISION OF YOUR BEST PATH

OPAROOM FANTESZAR
OPAROOM FANTESZAR
OPAROOM FANTESZAR

oh-par-oom fahn-tess-zar

Pronunciation File #17

BE ABLE TO ACCOMPLISH MORE IN LESS TIME

KHRONOS LOQUAR VIVIEL
KHRONOS LOQUAR VIVIEL
KHRONOS LOQUAR VIVIEL

crow-nose loh-kwawr viv-ee-el

Pronunciation File #18

REMEMBER AND INTERPRET YOUR DREAMS

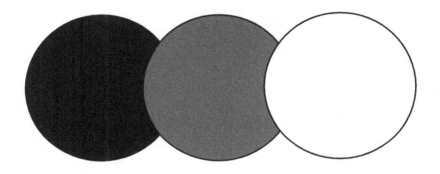

PEDLATZ
PEDLATZ
PEDLATZ

ped-lahtz

Pronunciation File #19

BECOME A LUCID DREAMER

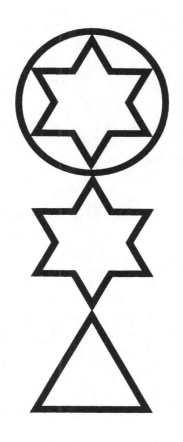

HUMAR RABATZ Q
HUMAR RABATZ Q
HUMAR RABATZ Q

hoo-mar rah-bats cue

Pronunciation File #20

UNLEASH AND DEVELOP YOUR CREATIVE & ARTISTIC ABILITIES

RABAA KALISH SUMAR
RABAA KALISH SUMAR
RABAA KALISH SUMAR

rah-bah kah-leesh sue-mar

Pronunciation File #21

RELATIONSHIPS AND INTERACTIONS WITH OTHERS

ATTRACT PEOPLE INTO YOUR LIFE THAT CAN HELP YOU

JATAASH WISEEF
JATAASH WISEEF
JATAASH WISEEF

jah-tahsh whis-eef

Pronunciation File #22

IMPROVE THE MOOD OF THE PEOPLE AROUND YOU

TOLOI KLONDISH
TOLOI KLONDISH
TOLOI KLONDISH

toh-loy klohn-dish

Pronunciation File #23

MAKE PEOPLE WARMER
TO YOU

QSUN
QSUN
QSUN

cue-sun

Pronunciation File #24

ENCOURAGE NEW HARMONIOUS FRIENDSHIPS

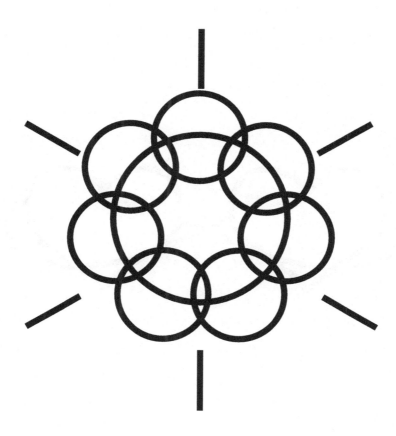

EIZENHAAR DLASHMIC
EIZENHAAR DLASHMIC
EIZENHAAR DLASHMIC

eye-zen-haar dlash-mic

Pronunciation File #25

ATTRACT A ROMANTIC RELATIONSHIP

JATAHSH LORNEY
JATAHSH LORNEY
JATAHSH LORNEY

jah-tahsh lorn-ey

Pronunciation File #26

ATTRACT YOUR TRUE LOVE / SOUL MATE

JATAHSH LAADAKAND
JATAHSH LAADAKAND
JATAHSH LAADAKAND

jah-tahsh lah-dah-kahn-dah

Pronunciation File #27

RECOVER LOST LOVE

BENEE JA
BENEE JA
BENEE JA

ben-ee jah

Pronunciation File #28

END A RELATIONSHIP EASILY

ZAR JASAWMUIR
ZAR JASAWMUIR
ZAR JASAWMUIR

zar jah-saw-muehr

Pronunciation File #29

MOTIVATE SOMEONE TO BECOME MORE COMPASSIONATE

VALACOT JASALOM
VALACOT JASALOM
VALACOT JASALOM

val-ah-kot jah-sah-lom

Pronunciation File #30

MOTIVATE SOMEONE TO BECOME LESS CRITICAL

VALACOT BLONTAY
VALACOT BLONTAY
VALACOT BLONTAY

val-ah-kot blon-taye

Pronunciation File #31

MOTIVATE SOMEONE TO BECOME MORE LOVING

VALACOT JASUPROM
VALACOT JASUPROM
VALACOT JASUPROM

val-ah-kot jah-sue-prahm

Pronunciation File #32

MOTIVATE SOMEONE TO BECOME MORE UNDERSTANDING

VALACOT KAZRUN
VALACOT KAZRUN
VALACOT KAZRUN

val-ah-kot kahz-ruhn

Pronunciation File #33

MOTIVATE SOMEONE STUCK IN A RUT TO CHANGE

VALACOT JUNDO
VALACOT JUNDO
VALACOT JUNDO

val-ah-kot june-doh

Pronunciation File #34

TURN EVERYONE'S FOCUSED ATTENTION TO YOU

ILLUMIN ASHKAJA
ILLUMIN ASHKAJA
ILLUMIN ASHKAJA

ill-loo-mihn ahsh-kah-jah

Pronunciation File #35

RECONCILE A RELATIONSHIP RIFT

DRONDA JASALASH
DRONDA JASALASH
DRONDA JASALASH

dron-dah jahsah-lash

Pronunciation File #36

REVEAL A PERSON'S HIDDEN AGENDA

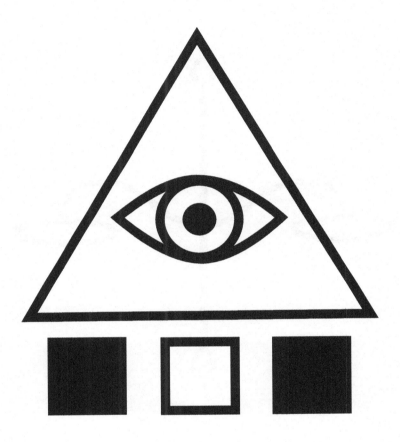

QPOC SALEEN
QPOC SALEEN
QPOC SALEEN

cue-pock sah-leen

Pronunciation File #37

ENSURE FAIR LEGAL DECISIONS

BRONTANA YITZER
BRONTANA YITZER
BRONTANA YITZER

brawn-tahn-ah yihtz-er

Pronunciation File #38

DEVELOP YOUR PSYCHIC ABILITIES

BECOME MORE CLAIRVOYANT

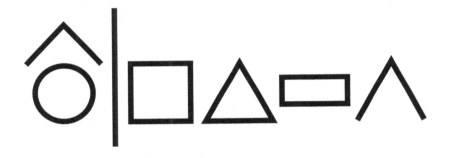

WISPAUN SHALONZ
WISPAUN SHALONZ
WISPAUN SHALONZ

whis-pawn shah-lohnz

Pronunciation File #39

BECOME MORE EMPATHIC

WISPAUN HOOKAMBA SAI
WISPAUN HOOKAMBA SAI
WISPAUN HOOKAMBA SAI

whis-pawn who-kahm-bah say

Pronunciation File #40

BECOME MORE AWARE OF AND COMPREHENDING OF A PERSON'S AURA

YONTONA VAUSHAUN QZA
YONTONA VAUSHAUN QZA
YONTONA VAUSHAUN QZA

yohn-tah-nah vawsh-awn cue-zah

Pronunciation File #41

COMMUNICATE WITH YOUR HIGHER SELF USING AUTOMATIC WRITING

VRANS XEKA KORBOSE
VRANS XEKA KORBOSE
VRANS XEKA KORBOSE

vrans zee-kah core-bohs

Pronunciation File #42

KNOW OTHER PEOPLE'S THOUGHTS

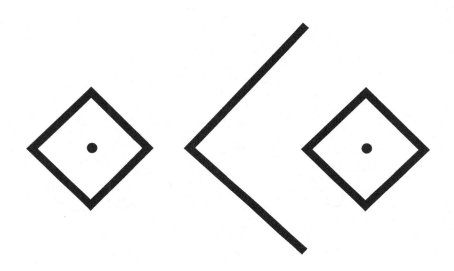

VAVA KADONG
VAVA KADONG
VAVA KADONG

vah-vah kuh-dong

Pronunciation File #43

MAGNIFY YOUR INTUITION

BARKALON DEE
BARKALON DEE
BARKALON DEE

bark-ah-lon dee

Pronunciation File #44

ACTIVATE & ENHANCE YOUR ABILITY TO ASTRAL PROJECT

YIZVAS XEOO EKATA
YIZVAS XEOO EKATA
YIZVAS XEOO EKATA

yhiz-vahss zee-oo eh-kah-tah

Pronunciation File #45

HEALTH

INCREASE YOUR DESIRE TO EAT HEALTHIER

COUPA ZING
COUPA ZING
COUPA ZING

coo-puh zing

Pronunciation File #46

DIMINISH ANXIETY, FEAR AND WORRY

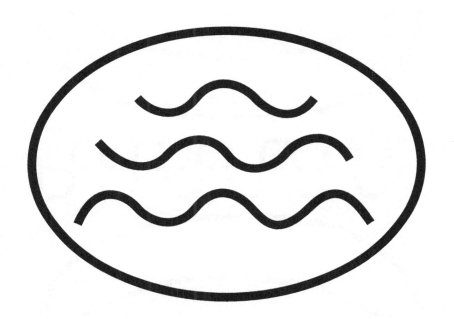

JAEL ALADAWON
JAEL ALADAWON
JAEL ALADAWON

jah-el ah-lahd-ah-whon

Pronunciation File #47

DIMINISH DEPRESSION

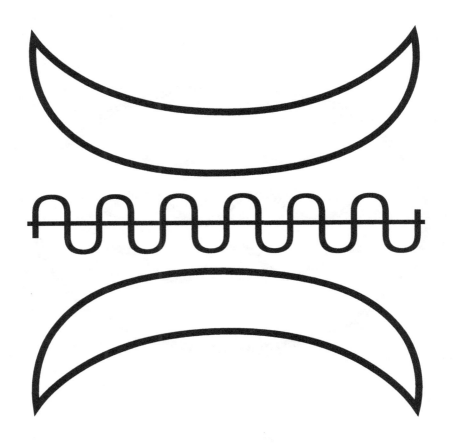

JAEL MARKEL
JAEL MARKEL
JAEL MARKEL

jah-el mar-kell

Pronunciation File #48

LESSEN EMOTIONAL PAIN OF GRIEF AFTER A LOSS

JAEL JULANARI
JAEL JULANARI
JAEL JULANARI

jah-el zhul-ahn-ahr-ee

Pronunciation File #49

DIMINISH PHYSICAL PAIN

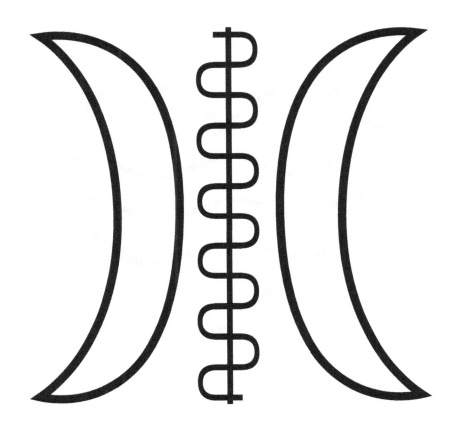

JAEL OMERICSOL
JAEL OMERICSOL
JAEL OMERICSOL

jah-el o-mehr-ick-sohl

Pronunciation File #50

STOP THINKING NEGATIVE THOUGHTS

SKOZ SKALAM
SKOZ SKALAM
SKOZ SKALAM

skoz skah-lam

Pronunciation File #51

IMPROVE YOUR MOOD

LERYLCEON
LERYLCEON
LERYLCEON

lehryl-cee-on

Pronunciation File #52

ATTRACT MORE POSITIVE AND SUPPORTIVE FRIENDS INTO YOUR LIFE

JATAASH MIRAKONDA
JATAASH MIRAKONDA
JATAASH MIRAKONDA

jah-tahsh meer-ah-conda

Pronunciation File #53

FEEL MOTIVATED
TO EXERCISE

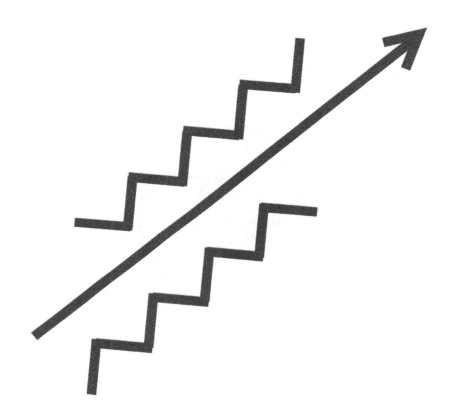

SPARLACLE TORAN
SPARLACLE TORAN
SPARLACLE TORAN

spar-lack-el tor-ahn

Pronunciation File #54

HEAL YOUR HEART FROM AN EMOTIONAL WOUND

SOOLASEE JA GRAASON
SOOLASEE JA GRAASON
SOOLASEE JA GRAASON

soo-lah-see jah grah-sohn

Pronunciation File #55

INCREASE METABOLISM AND DESIRE TO LOSE WEIGHT

TA RA ZERAM
TA RA ZERAM
TA RA ZERAM

tah rah zehr-am

Pronunciation File #56

INCREASE YOUR PHYSICAL ENERGY, STRENGTH AND VITALITY

LODOSH WIZTAR
LODOSH WIZTAR
LODOSH WIZTAR

lohd-ahsh whiz-tahr

Pronunciation File #57

SPEED HEALING FROM A PHYSICAL INJURY

VASTAN SOOLASEE BORGATEE
VASTAN SOOLASEE BORGATEE
VASTAN SOOLASEE BORGATEE

vahss-tahn soo-lah-see bore-guh-tee

Pronunciation File #58

SPEED HEALING FROM A PHYSICAL ILLNESS

VASTAN SOOLASEE VORDAR
VASTAN SOOLASEE VORDAR
VASTAN SOOLASEE VORDAR

vahss-tahn soo-lah-see vor-dahr

Pronunciation File #59

ACCELERATE HEALING OF A DISEASE

VASTAN SOOLASEE FIZ
VASTAN SOOLASEE FIZ
VASTAN SOOLASEE FIZ

vahss-tahn soo-lah-see fihz

Pronunciation File #60

ACTIVATE ENERGY INSIDE OF YOU TO HEAL OTHERS

JAAZ QBONDA
JAAZ QBONDA
JAAZ QBONDA

jaaz cue-bohn-dah

Pronunciation File #61

SLEEP PEACEFULLY AND GET A GOOD NIGHT'S REST

AASHKADAR KURAZ
AASHKADAR KURAZ
AASHKADAR KURAZ

ahsh-kah-dar coo-rahz

Pronunciation File #62

ACTIVATE REJUVENATION OF YOUR BODY TO A MORE YOUTHFUL STATE

QWEX VISH YONZ
QWEX VISH YONZ
QWEX VISH YONZ

qwhex vish yohnz

Pronunciation File #63

ACTIVATE REJUVENATION OF YOUR MIND TO THE QUICKNESS OF YOUTH

QWEX ZADATTA KABON
QWEX ZADATTA KABON
QWEX ZADATTA KABON

qwhex zah-daht-tuh kah-bon

Pronunciation File #64

ACTIVATE REJUVENATION OF YOUR SKIN TO A MORE YOUTHFUL STATE

QWEX SILANTI YONZ
QWEX SILANTI YONZ
QWEX SILANTI YONZ

qwhex-sill-ahn-tee yohnz

Pronunciation File #65

ERASE A MEMORY YOU DO NOT WISH TO REMEMBER

HAVATOR BLAASH
HAVATOR BLAASH
HAVATOR BLAASH

hahv-ah-tour blaash

Pronunciation File #66

MONEY & SUCCESS

PROPEL YOUR BUSINESS OR PROJECT TO TAKE OFF

FJAR SKOS
FJAR SKOS
FJAR SKOS

fuhjahr skoss

Pronunciation File #67

ATTRACT FINANCIAL SUPPORT FOR A PROJECT

JATAASH MORATAWN PURATONDE
JATAASH MORATAWN PURATONDE
JATAASH MORATAWN PURATONDE

jah-tahsh moor-ah-tawn pyoor-ah-tohn-dey

Pronunciation File #68

HAVE MONEY COME TO YOU UNEXPECTEDLY

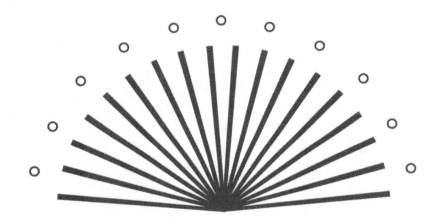

FEIZ NATHAAN
FEIZ NATHAAN
FEIZ NATHAAN

fee-eyz nahth-ahn

Pronunciation File #69

INCREASE YOUR INCOME

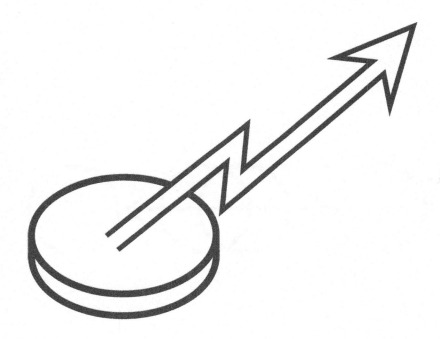

ORBANDA ALAMOZ
ORBANDA ALAMOZ
ORBANDA ALAMOZ

ohr-bahwn-dah al-ah-mahz

Pronunciation File #70

MAKE YOUR MONTHLY INCOME GO FURTHER

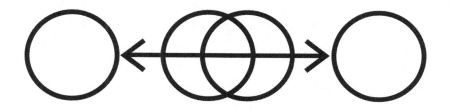

ALAMOZ USAS
ALAMOZ USAS
ALAMOZ USAS

al-ah-mahz you-sahss

Pronunciation File #71

CAREER & SCHOOL

BECOME MORE INTELLIGENT AND RETAIN KNOWLEDGE EASIER

QUIALANTRA KA
QUIALANTRA KA
QUIALANTRA KA

ki-ah-lahn-trah kah

Pronunciation File #72

REMEMBER WHAT YOU STUDY AND DO WELL ON THE TEST

VALAZIX KA
VALAZIX KA
VALAZIX KA

vah-lah-zix kah

Pronunciation File #73

EASILY LEARN A NEW SKILL OR TALENT

QWASATAR KA
QWASATAR KA
QWASATAR KA

kwah-suh-tar kah

Pronunciation File #74

BE BETTER ORGANIZED

STEEKA
STEEKA
STEEKA

stee-kah

Pronunciation File #75

OBTAIN IDEAL EMPLOYMENT IN YOUR PREFERRED FIELD

SUDAS BORLATAY VICAN
SUDAS BORLATAY VICAN
SUDAS BORLATAY VICAN

soo-dahs boor-lah-tay vih-kahn

Pronunciation File #76

HAVE YOUR TALENT NOTICED BY PEOPLE THAT CAN HELP YOU

ZERAT TAKROK SIRACOSS
ZERAT TAKROK SIRACOSS
ZERAT TAKROK SIRACOSS

zehr-aht tahk-roc seer-ah-cahss

Pronunciation File #77

START A SUCCESSFUL BUSINESS FROM YOUR PASSION

ORCH KARONDAR POTON
ORCH KARONDAR POTON
ORCH KARONDAR POTON

orch kah-ron-dar poe-tohn

Pronunciation File #78

BE A BETTER PUBLIC SPEAKER

SWARL TAJAZ
SWARL TAJAZ
SWARL TAJAZ

swarl tuh-jahz

Pronunciation File #79

CREATE AN IMMEDIATE ACTION ENERGY

GAIN WHATEVER YOU NEED TO OVERCOME AN EMERGENCY

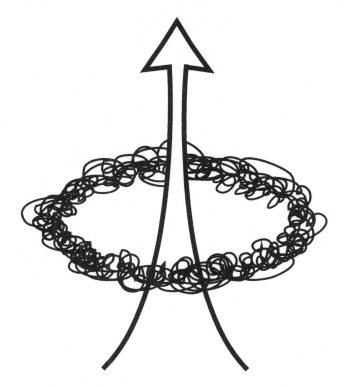

ELOHIM OOTAME
ELOHIM OOTAME
ELOHIM OOTAME

el-oh-heem oo-tah-mee

Pronunciation File #80

INVOKE A CIRCLE OF PROTECTION FROM PSYCHIC ATTACKS

ZAKA XERAMZEY
ZAKA XERAMZEY
ZAKA XERAMZEY

zahk-ah zee-ram-zey

Pronunciation File #81

INVOKE A CIRCLE OF PROTECTION FROM PHYSICAL VIOLENCE

ZAKA WZRAMZEY
ZAKA WZRAMZEY
ZAKA WZRAMZEY

zahk-ah whiz-ram-zey

Pronunciation File #82

MAKE AN ADVERSARY OR ANTAGONIST LOSE INTEREST IN YOU

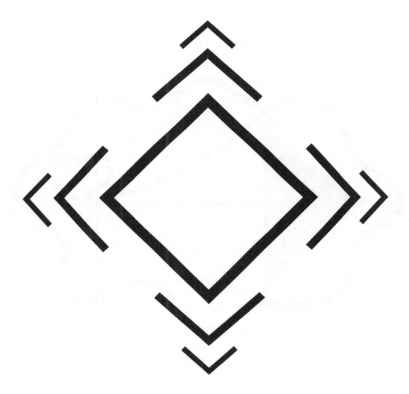

AKA WESSAN
AKA WESSAN
AKA WESSAN

ah-kah whes-sahn

Pronunciation File #83

CALM ANGER IN YOURSELF
OR OTHERS

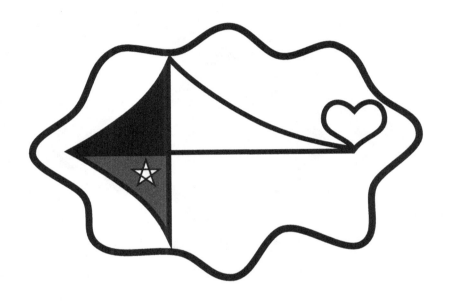

TALIALEE
TALIALEE
TALIALEE

tah-lee-ah-lee

Pronunciation File #84

EXCEL IN A COMPETITION

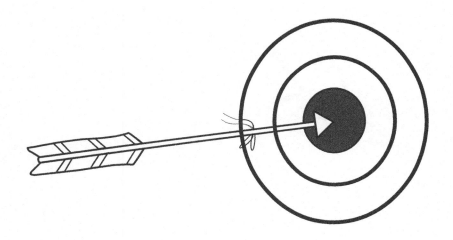

SHAMARIZ AKAWI
SHAMARIZ AKAWI
SHAMARIZ AKAWI

shaa-mar-iz ah-kah-wee

Pronunciation File #85

END A DISPUTE OR ARGUMENT

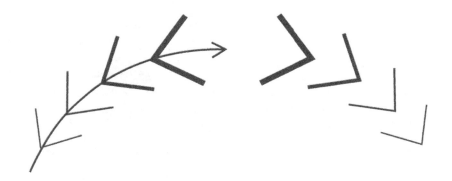

NANTOR QKALON
NANTOR QKALON
NANTOR QKALON

nahn-toor cue-kah-lohn

Pronunciation File #86

DISINTEREST AND DEFLECT UNWANTED ATTENTION

ZAUP
ZAUP
ZAUP

zahp

Pronunciation File #87

RAPIDLY CHANGE YOUR LIFE'S REALITY

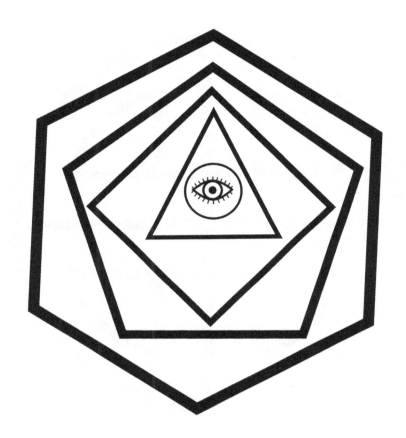

VOLONDO PARTANA
VOLONDO PARTANA
VOLONDO PARTANA

voh-lohn-doh pahr-tahn-ah

Pronunciation File #88

COALESCE, CONCENTRATE AND AMPLIFY YOUR AURIC POWER

ZONTA VARBON
ZONTA VARBON
ZONTA VARBON

zohn-tuh var-bohn

Pronunciation File #89

SECTION III

INTRODUCTION TO ADVANCED MAGICKAL WORDS OF CELESTINE LIGHT

his section is intended to introduce you to some of the more advanced castings that can be done in Celestine Light that also employ Words of Power and sigils. Solely saying the Words of Power and looking at the sigil will have beneficial effects for the purpose desired for anyone with good intent. However, the power and length of time the effect lasts will be greatly enhanced by either additional casting rituals, use of specific magickal tools, the power and purity of the auric field of the person or people invoking the power, or all three of those.

In some of the listings that follow the additional actions that can be taken to enhance the effect may be simple enough to be detailed and useful for anyone seeking that purpose. Others may involve more complex additional actions that are beyond the scope of this book.

Lastly, although many people may be unhappy with this reality, magick of the light simply works better for the person activating the magick who has more light within their soul. Your character, how you live your life, the respect and consideration you give other people, how you treat your body and the respect you give to yourself, how you invest your free time, and even the things you choose to eat, all contribute to the purity and power of the light that emanates from you.

Ultimately, the purity of the light you hold within you is a major factor in the power of any work of Celestine magick that you invoke. All of the higher level magickal words and sigils found in Section III, require a higher level of light to be fully effective.

LEVITATE AN OBJECT

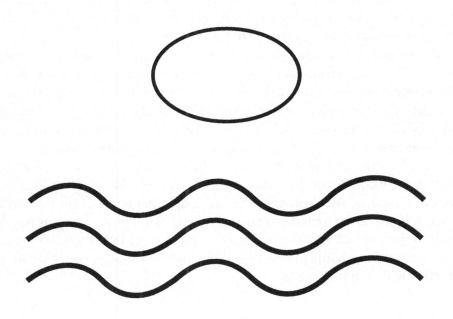

KEL ARZ
KEL ARZ
KEL ARZ

kell arzz

Pronunciation File #90

This is higher magick even though Yeshua made it seem so simple in the **Oracles of Celestine Light**. An essential requirement is complete, undistracted focus. The other essential requirement is the ability to tightly concentrate your own auric field inside your body, then send it in highly concentrated form through your arm and shoot it out your hand. Lastly, if your hand is holding a wand, it will amplify and help tightly focus the auric energy bursting out of your hand.

If someone has a great interest in this particular act of magick, they should first become proficient in the simple movements of Telekinesis. Most people can begin moving light objects within the first 15 minutes of practice with the techniques outlined in my *Telekinesis* book. Once you are proficient with those and can move light objects within a minute or two of focusing, you are ready to step up to levitation of objects.

Just like with telekinesis, begin with lighter objects and do it as it was done in the examples in the Oracles where you are holding an object at the apex of its ascent after you have thrown it up. That is the point that even a heavy object is for a moment virtually weightless before it begins its fall back to the ground. It is the best time to put a force of levitation upon it to prevent it from being pulled back down by gravity. Start your levitation practice with juggling scarfs.

SUMMON A PERSON TO YOU OR LEAD YOU TO THEM

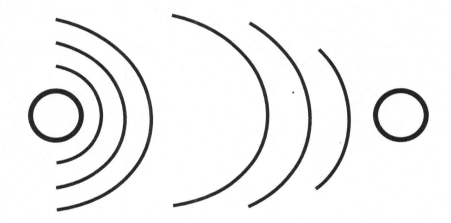

USASAALOO BARONDE
USASAALOO BARONDE
USASAALOO BARONDE

yoo-sah-sah-ah-loo bah-ron-day

Pronunciation File #91

These Words of Power work fairly well on their own or combined with the sigil. If the person is someone close to you, the results will be even better if you have a piece of their recently worn clothing or jewelry you can hold between your two hands as you say the Words of Power and look at the sigil.

If it is someone you are not close to or may not even know, additional magickal rituals will help, including saying the Words of Power and looking at the sigil just before you retire for the evening, and then keep a white candle lit in your room as you fall asleep at night. This will lead to night visions showing you where the person is located. This step may also be used with someone you are close to in addition to holding their clothing or jewelry.

Do keep in mind that this also works both ways - people you are searching for can be pulled to find you just as you can be led to find them.

BE LED TO A LOST OR HIDDEN OBJECT

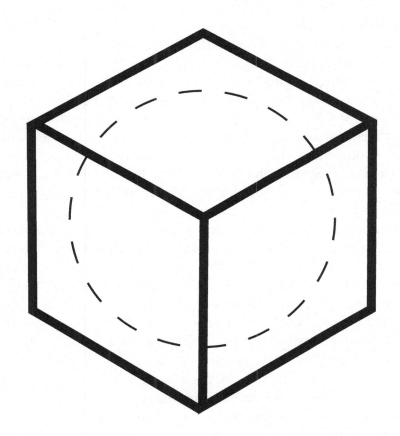

ISH JULALONTAY
ISH JULALONTAY
ISH JULALONTAY

ish zhul-ah-lohn-tay

Pronunciation File #92

I recently had an opportunity to employ these Words of Power and their matching sigil, along with the additional actions necessary to optimize the success.

I dislike having to talk on the phone as it disrupts my flow during the day. Therefore, I do not own a cell phone and we do not have a land line phone for our house. My wife's cell phone is our primary way of communicating by telephone with the outside world. But her phone was put down somewhere that nobody could remember and we couldn't ring it as it was no longer on due to a depleted battery. It became an escalating, but still minor irritation the longer it remained missing. We looked everywhere for it, multiple times, without being rewarded for our efforts.

Days went by and at one point I actually needed the phone. I was irritated enough that I decided that it was time to find it. I called my wife and invited a Celestine friend that was at the house to join us, as I pulled out a sheet of paper with the sigil and Words of Power printed on it for finding a lost object.

We linked arms around each others waists in a circle and said the Words of Power three times aloud while looking at the sigil. We said the words with a bit of passionate emphasis as we were at the point that we really wanted to find the phone! Passion always makes magick work better.

Immediately afterward I held a six inch long naturally double-terminated quartz crystal between my two hands. It is one of my favorite magickal tools. I closed my eyes and silently asked to be led to the phone. I spun around in place in a slow circle paying great attention to what the crystal felt like as I went 360 degrees around in the circle. There was a point that I felt a faint thickening of the air as I passed the crystal through it. It was almost like suddenly being caught in a magnetic pull or a Star trek tractor beam. I did the circle two more times and confirmed the pull of the crystal when it was pointing in a very specific direction.

I continued this method as I walked through the house following the pulling signals of the crystal. Each time I entered a new room I would slowly spin in a circle to determine what direction to proceed.

Within three minutes I had located the phone in a place we never looked and probably never would have. It was on a closet shelf in the master bedroom but completely hidden beneath the bottom of a long dress hanging above it. We have a small ironing board that drops down from the wall in the closet. After I found the phone my wife remembered absentmindedly putting it on that shelf while she was ironing one of her dresses. Thank you magick!

DISCERN AN ENERGY VAMPIRE

BORMAI VORDAR
BORMAI VORDAR
BORMAI VORDAR

boor-mey voor-dar

Pronunciation File #93

Energy Vampires get their auric energy not from actions of positive self improvement, but rather from sucking it out of others. Just like the thief who steals other peoples possessions because they perceive that to be easier than working a job to earn the money to buy the items, Energy Vampires find it far easier to just suck energy from other people than to have to make efforts to create their own.

They are bad dudes or dudettes, but that is not the image they usually project publicly. However, their private persona is often quite different than their public face. Where they may be charming and feign interest in someone in public and even be considered one of the nicest people because they seem to listen and empathize, in private they will typically disdain the same people who admired them.

The fate of family members out of the public eye is often much worse. It is from them that most Energy Vampires will focus their efforts to drain energy from an unwilling victim. Where they may have seemed the epitome of calm and reason in public, in private they will often start arguments, usually over trivial things. The more they can stir things up and upset their victim, the more energy that is available for them to suck. To that end they typically do not hold back, but make every effort to traumatize their victim with harsh and demeaning words, yelling, screaming and ranting on and on endlessly and in all too many instances, with physical violence.

People often wonder why victims of ongoing domestic abuse didn't simply walk away long ago. While there may be many contributing reasons such as children or family pressures, in many cases the victim was just too beat down, emotionally, spiritually, mentally, physically and energetically to think clearly or to act in their own best interest. These are the conditions Energy Vampires thrive upon and go out of their way to create.

The Words of Power and sigils for discerning an Energy Vampire are hugely helpful for anyone contemplating getting into a romantic or business relationship with another person, or even associating casually with them. However, there are a couple of extra steps required.

While it may be possible to discern and verify whether someone is an Energy Vampire by just using the Words of Power and the sigil, a more certain method requires you to use an article of their recently worn clothing, or an item they touch frequently such as their favorite pen or piece of jewelry. Take the item and hold it between your two hands as you say the Words of Power and look at the sigil. You will immediately get a feeling in your heart or a knowing in your mind and often times both, that will clearly let you know whether that person is an Energy Vampire or not.

I should make mention of another rarer type of Energy Vampire and that is the involuntary one. Normal Energy Vampires are perfectly happy the way they are. They like causing distress in others and feeding off their energy. Involuntary Energy Vampires realize that they have that affect on others - of sucking their energy, but it is not something they wish to do and they are typically sad when they realize it has occurred.

These are the type of individuals that you will find your mood suddenly dampened for no apparent reason when you are around them. They are not fighting or arguing with you. In fact, they are probably being very nice to you, yet you still feel a negative energy when you are around them. In these situations, with these type of unwilling Energy Vampires, using the #94 Words of Power and sigil will be very effective and allow you to be around the Energy Vampire without being negatively affected.

NEUTRALIZE NEGATIVE ENERGY

TA RA ZERRAM
TA RA ZERRAM
TA RA ZERRAM

tah rah zehr-ahm

Pronunciation File #94

If you know you are going to be in a situation or circumstance where you will likely encounter negative energy from the words, actions or intent of other people, take a piece of gold jewelry you are going to be wearing, the higher karat gold the better, hold it between the palms of your hands and say the Words of Power aloud three times while also looking at the sigil.

This will temporarily enchant the piece of jewelry and effectively shield you from being affected by the negative energy emanating from the words, actions or intent of others. This is a very simple form of enchantment and it will wear off within a day and often within a few hours, depending upon your own auric power, focus and sincere desire when you imbued it.

REFLECT A PSYCHIC ATTACK BACK UPON THE ATTACKER

TAKROTH XERRAMZA
TAKROTH XERRAMZA
TAKROTH XERRAMZA

tahk-rawth zehr-ram-zah

Pronunciation File #95

To get the best results this should be a more involved spell. The Words of Power and sigil will have some beneficial effect but are only a part of a larger group of magickal actions necessary to create a powerful reflection. While the downside is this is not an instant piece of potent Celestine magick, the good side is it does have a long lasting and powerful effect when the additional actions are incorporated.

Written instructions for the procedure are insufficient. An Adept of Celestine Light is required to educate and demonstrate the techniques and ritual in person to insure it is done properly for maximum effectiveness. Because this directly affects another person, the caster desiring the reflection must themselves be in a place of calm and in harmony with the Celestine Light. Hence use this one with the caution that the Words of Power and sigil will only have slight affect on their own.

CREATE A CLOAKING BUBBLE OF DISINTEREST AND INVISIBILITY

YIZATAZ
YIZATAZ
YIZATAZ

yhiz-ah-tahz

Pronunciation File #96

There are instances when you may not want to leave a social or public event, but you also do not want to draw notice to yourself, or in particular if you are a woman, be hit upon by men. This is a nice, easy to remember single Word of Power that effectively makes people pass right over you when they are looking around as if you were not even there.

You can say the word Yizataz aloud, whisper it under your breath or even just think it in your mind. Of course you also have to do your part. If you stand up on the stage everyone is going to be looking at you. But if you do not purposefully draw attention to yourself by your actions, speech, or looks you give people, Yizataz will keep you fairly anonymous and unnoticed.

If you want even more success with this purpose, say Yizataz three times aloud while looking at the sigil before you go to a place you do not wish to be noticed. Once you are there you can reinforce the energy as needed by occasionally uttering Yizataz, quietly.

If you feel you need still more power to this purpose, imbue the Yizataz energy into a piece of jewelry you will be wearing by holding it tightly between your palms when you speak the word aloud three times while looking at the sigil. The jewelry will then strongly radiate the energy of Yizataz for the next two to four hours, depending upon how well you imbued it with your focus and sincere desire.

MAKE AN ENEMY OR ATTACKER AFRAID OF YOU

AKA TROMBO QYAT
AKA TROMBO QYAT
AKA TROMBO QYAT

ah-kah trom-bo cue-yat

Pronunciation File #97

These Words of Power alone are quite powerful if used in a situation as it is occurring. The more energetic and pure the casters auric field is, the more potent and noticeable the effect will be. But even the weakest most timid person can have a modicum of results using nothing more than the Words of Power Aka Trombo Qyat in a situation of need. The words can be spoken aloud or even said in your mind with equal effect. Say them three times to maximize your results.

In more advanced Celestine Light Magick, additional rituals and procedures will invoke longer lasting and more powerful effects.

BE LED TO A DIMENSIONAL DOORWAY

VAVEL ONDIX
VAVEL ONDIX
VAVEL ONDIX

vah-vell ohn-dicks

Pronunciation File #98

Dimensional doorways are almost always found in very close proximity to Energy Vortexes and vortexes are much easier to locate from a distance. Doorways are often in dark places like caves, dense woods, or even just small shadowed depressions in a rock face.

Once you are at the vortex, a number of methods can be successfully used to locate the dimensional doorway. They should be used after you have said the *Words of Power* three times aloud and looked at the sigil.

If there is a dimensional doorway present, it will usually be within 100 yards of the vortex. Occasionally you will find the doorway as much as a quarter of a mile or more away, but that is unusual. Following the sensation or signals generated by pendulums, pointed quartz crystals held between your hands, or even just going by your feelings and where you are drawn to, will lead you to discover the location of the dimensional doorway, if there is one present.

Only about 1 out of 50 vortexes have a dimensional doorway near them. In other words, while you will always find energy vortexes, either positive, negative or both, near dimensional doorways, you will not always find dimensional doorways near energy vortexes.

WARNING: If you happen to come upon a dimensional doorway that is open, it will appear like an electric blue spinning tunnel. Run away as fast as you can! Under NO circumstances should you enter the dimensional portal no matter how strong you think your magick is! These are entrances to other worlds that are almost all exceptionally different, harsh and more unforgiving than ours. And many of the creatures that dwell there make the worst on Earth seem tame by comparison. Save your life and keep out!

BE LED TO AN ENERGY VORTEX

SOOLASEE GRAASON
SOOLASEE GRAASON
SOOLASEE GRAASON

sool-lah-see grah-sun

Pronunciation File #99

The best tool here might surprise you - it's Google Earth! The first step in locating an energy vortex, whether positive energy or negative, is to narrow down the search area. You can use a detailed topographic map such as USGS quadrangle maps and a pendulum to scry a pinpoint location, but that requires its own skill in using a pendulum and scrying.

An easier and quicker method, at least for me is to use Google Earth. I open up Google Earth and zoom in on an area I would like to investigate about the size of a typical county. I won't know yet if there is even a vortex there, but I want to investigate it to see.

I begin by saying the Words of Power three times aloud and looking at the sigil. Then I start looking closer at the area on Google Earth. Vortexes are most often found on hilltops or other promontories, or near other unusual natural features such as waterfalls. However, they also can be found out in the middle of an empty field, amongst a forest of trees, or even out in the middle of a body of water. They will often cause an aberration compared to the surrounding area. Sometimes this can be seen by zooming in on Google Earth. It can include things like a small discolored patch of earth, a circular pattern in bedrock, a small, natural, circular clearing in an otherwise dense forest, or the opposite, a small circular stand of trees in an otherwise treeless location. Almost all oases of spring-fed water in desert climates will have vortexes.

As I look at Google Earth images I will be strongly drawn to certain locations. Even when I try to meander somewhere else on the pictographic map I am almost compelled to go back and look at that particular spot.

That lets me know there is a vortex nearby. Sometimes I can determine the exact location simply by looking at the Google Earth images. Some places become obvious because of their nearby physical features such as waterfalls. More often, if it seems to be interesting enough to invest the time, it will require a trip in the field to determine the exact location.

For me, once I am within a quarter of mile or so of the vortex I will strongly feel its tingling, swirling energy interacting with my own auric field and will easily be able to locate it simply by walking toward the direction it feels strongest. Once I am there I can visually see it like a swirling tornado. Positive vortexes will be in pale colors of white, gold, and other light colors and hues, along with lots of golden sparkles. Negative energy vortexes will be in darker colors and hues, have no sparkles, and will be spinning much more lethargically.

If you do not yet have that level of sensitivity I recommend bringing a wand or your favorite quartz crystal or spiral shell. These all make excellent vortex locators. Hold your chosen item in your *left* hand and point it in front of you with your arm loosely and comfortably extended. Turn in a 360 degree circle. There will be a point that you feel as if a subtle unseen force is grabbing on to your wand and pulling you toward it. Just continue to follow the pull and you will soon be at the vortex.

If you cannot see it visually and want to determine whether it is conducting positive or negative energy, simply pay attention to how you feel when you are near it or in it. Do you feel more energetic, optimistic and uplifted or sad or down for no apparent reason.

You also need to be very careful if the vortex is anywhere near a cliff or someplace you could fall and hurt yourself. Even people who completely do not believe in such things as energy vortexes are immediately physically affected by them. The stronger the vortex, the stronger the effect, especially if you are standing inside the vortex. Because the vortexes swirl around and around, your body tends to start involuntarily begin to swirl around and around too. You can consciously stop it, but if you are not putting that type of mental brake on, your body's natural inclination will be to move with the flow of the vortex. If you are on a flat piece of safe ground that's no problem. But if you are in any type of precarious location, you could easily lose your balance and fall, so be careful around vortexes!

TRANSFER ENERGY FROM AN ENCHANTMENT INTO AN OBJECT

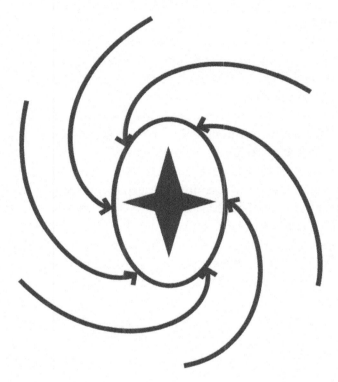

RACSAA BINGGALI TORMONDAI
RACSAA BINGGALI TORMONDAI
RACSAA BINGGALI TORMONDAI

raac-saah bing-gah-lie tor-mahn-day

Pronunciation File #100

This is a higher level of Celestine Light magick that can only be done under certain circumstances. So what follows is just being given for general informational purposes.

In addition to the Words of Power and sigil, a powerful enchantment requires a custom written spell specifically for the purpose of the enchantment. When crafting the spell it requires a thorough knowledge of the hundreds of universal energies to know which ones to call in for the enchantment.

Many potent, long-lasting enchantments also require the assistance of angels and there are hundreds of them. Each angel has a focused specialty that is their stewardship. The correct angel or angels must be called upon in the written and spoken spell.

For more than transitory effect, it also requires a quality object for the energy of the enchantment to be imbued into, such as a piece of gold jewelry or a crystal or specially attuned stone.

There are also secret techniques that must be applied to the object during the enchanting process and these will vary depending upon the type of object being enchanted.

Lastly, the caster of the enchantment needs to have considerable auric power or the casting must be done by three, six or twelve Celestines gathered into a Circle of Power specifically for that purpose.

INITIATE A CIRCLE
OF POWER

ZARZAN ZARTAC ZARSAAZ
ZARZAN ZARTAC ZARSAAZ
ZARZAN ZARTAC ZARSAAZ

zar-zan zar-tahc zar-sahz

Pronunciation File #101

This is another item given just for general informational purposes. Circles of Power can be created by a group of three, six or twelve Celestines gathered in harmony and unison for a single focused purpose. The purposes can be quite varied, everything from creating an enchantment to imbue into an object, to casting a spell to affect something small or something on a much larger scale.

The Words of Power are spoken to initiate the Circle of Power followed by the specific spell and actions required to activate the energy. In many instances there are certain times of the month such as a full moon, when Circles of Power have their energy even further amplified. Very rare and extremely powerful Circles of Power can be activated during rare celestial events such as lunar or solar eclipses.

SECTION IV

PRELUDE TO THE NAMES AND
SIGILS OF ANGELS

o you believe in angels? If not, start calling upon those that you do not believe in, using their name and unique sigil, and you will soon become a believer! The sequel to this book will be all about how to call on the power of angels to help you in your life by focusing upon their sigil and invoking their name.

There are over one hundred angels very actively involved with helping the people of this world, irrespective of their religion or creed, because that is what they have been tasked to do. ***However, it's exceptionally important to call upon the right angel to get the best results*** and this is something very few people know and utilize. Each angel has a specific stewardship, an area of responsibility and expertise. Knowing the correct angel to call upon to help you in your need insures you will actually open a conduit to the angelic power and not just be uselessly talking to a blank wall. It also invokes the optimum energy required to succeed.

Whereas many of the sigils in *Words of Power & Transformation* have some level of complexity and recognizable symbolic flair to them, sigils of angels are ancient and visually distinctive in nature from other types of sigils. Some are clearly symbolic in their representation. Others are in many ways like the signature of the angel. Most parts of the signature of angelic sigils can be drawn in a single line without lifting the pen off the paper, just as most people would write their signature, other than when dotting i's or crossing t's. Though imperfect derivatives can be found in many sources from modern to medieval, we are fortunate in Celestine

Light to be able to call upon the angels using the most pure and perfect form of their sigil. Here are some examples:

Archangel Michael

Archangel Gabriel

Angel Laconda

Angel Bromati

When invoking angels, it is important to remember that they are higher beings of light. They respond to people of any faith that are striving to be good people and live in the light. Angels are keepers of special powers and energies bestowed by the divine creator. They are tasked with specific responsibilities and have a stewardship to provide those specific energies when called upon for a sincere and honorable purpose, by people of any faith, age, sex, creed or color.

Using the name and sigil of an angel is a short cut to gain access to the energies, forces and powers they are stewards over. While the same effect might be obtained by a long involved prayer or repeated prayers, calling upon the proper angel based upon their stewardship and using their name and sigil, immediately cuts to the chase of the issue with a laser focus.

Like the sun and the rain that are available for all people regardless of their beliefs, angels awaken to heed the call of their name and the energy focus of their sigil, as long as the purpose of the person invoking them is not intended to hurt another person and is for an honorable and honest purpose of light.

APPENDIX A

PRONUNCIATION SOUND FILES FOR ALL WORDS OF POWER

ith magickal Words of Power, knowing how to correctly pronounce the words is only the first step. For maximum affect and speed you also need to have the correct inflection and put the emphasis on the correct syllables. To aid you in this important aspect please follow the link below to hear a sound file of all the Words of Power covered in this book. You will have the opportunity to hear the correct pronunciation, inflection and emphasis to give you the maximum success using the Celestine Light Words of Power. The pronunciation file number corresponds to the number for the item in the book.

www.embrosewyn.com/wordsofpower101

If you are reading an eBook you should be able to simply click on the link above to go to the sound file page. If you are reading a paperback version, or if the link in your eBook doesn't work, simply copy and paste the URL above into any Internet connected browser.

Caution: The Celestine Light Words of Power calls in powerful magick of the light. They should not be used with their correct pronunciation and inflection by anyone that has not been prepared by the knowledge in this book.

Please respect the copyright of this book
and especially do not share or post the sound file page URL.
Be safe; there are consequences to the misuse of magick.

APPENDIX B

EXAMPLES OF USE OF WORDS OF POWER FROM THE ORACLES OF CELESTINE LIGHT

he Oracles of Celestine Light, a scriptural record of the life and teachings of Yeshua of Nazareth and his wife Miriam of Magdela, contain several notable examples of the use of words of power. Following are some of these excerpts.

Levitation of a Rock and of Miriam
Vivus 36:51-66

(Comment: There are no actual Words of Power recorded here, but both Yeshua and Miriam used them in this instance. However, it was forbidden to record them in writing. They are only allowed to be passed down by word of mouth from one Adept to another.)

51 Taking up a fist-size rock, Yeshua threw it up into the sky. Everyone watched as it reached its apex and began to fall again to the Earth. But when it was at the height of their heads, it just stopped and remained standing still in the air, neither rising nor falling.

52 Then the rock rose slowly until it was about the height of two men above the ground and remained motionless.

53 Yeshua taught them, "To each of you and all the true Children of Light is given the power to know the thoughts of men and have influence upon them, to know the thoughts of one another without speaking, to

heal your body and the bodies of others of all manner of infirmities, to call upon the Sun or the storms, to see events of the future that will unfold, to have slight control of time and the ability to change the essence of one thing to another.

54 "And like this rock or the tree cast upon the mountain or the mountain upon the sea, it has been given to Adepts of the Celestine Light to have the power to make rise that which the world would say cannot rise and to make fall that which the world would say cannot fall.

55 "All these powers and more I have not spoken of sleep inside of you, waiting to be awakened by your confidence and faith. Are there any of you who have that confidence and faith today?"

56 Notwithstanding their amazement at the rock that hung still suspended in the air, most everyone nodded their heads affirmatively, and Cephas said, "I know my faith in Elohim is like a mountain. Of my confidence, I am not so sure, for though I believe if you say we can do these things, then surely we can do them, convincing myself that I actually can is another net of fish."

57 Yeshua pointed at the rock above and said unto him, "The test is easy, brother Cephas. Fetch that rock from the sky however you can with the powers manifested by your confidence and faith."

58 The eyes of Cephas became very large as he contemplated the challenge before him, but he went into intense concentration and tried to will the rock back to Earth but it would not move. He excused his lack of success, saying, "It is by your power that it remains where it is, and surely I cannot be greater than you, no matter the strength of my confidence or faith."

59 Yeshua answered him, saying, "By my power it floats in the sky, but as soon as any one of you manifests the barest power to move it, so it shall be moved as you will."

60 Once again, Cephas concentrated upon moving the stone to the ground, but once more, he was disappointed.

61 Others came forward and made a similar attempt, until five had tried and failed.

62 Then Miriam stepped forward and bowed her head to Yeshua, saying, "I will fetch the stone, my Lord, that my brothers and sisters may know with assurance that the powers we have been given are as you have said, that their confidence and faith may be emboldened by what they see me do, even as I have been emboldened by the many miracles I have seen

you do."

63 With that, she made as if to step upon an invisible step, and in a heartbeat, her body rose off the ground until she hovered before the stone and gently grasping it in her hand, she descended slowly and gracefully back to the Earth, until standing beside Yeshua, she opened her hand and presented the stone to him.

64 There were gasps of overwhelming surprise and awe, for this was an ability of the Celestine Light; greater than any had ever seen. Yeshua explained, "Marvel not at this, for you can do likewise, if along with your faith, your confidence is borne from a foundation of knowledge of the mysteries of Celestine Light, as it is for Miriam.

65 "To hold a stone floating in the air or to rise above the walls of the prisons that would hold you, or walk across the lake that would impede you, are merely manifestations of one of the abilities Elohim gave each of the Children of Light to be used with prudence and thankfulness by those who grow in knowledge of the secrets of Celestine Light and become Adepts of the highest.

66 "Now I reveal these things to you that you will open your thoughts to the magnificence that you can become, for only by thinking of yourself in greater terms than you have can you begin to become greater than you have been."

Healing the Ancient City of Trye from the Pall of Dark Energy
Vivus 64:102-147

102 Looking to Cephas, he asked, "Brother Cephas, would you please hand out to each person the tools I asked you to bring?"

103 Nodding in acknowledgment, Cephas took a plain wooden box out from within his personal backsack. Opening it, he removed a linen wrap and, unraveling it, revealed many long, clear quartz crystal wands.

104 Cephas cupped the linen with the wands close to him and then went around the circle, handing one to each person including Yeshua. When he returned to his spot in the circle, he held the last one. Had Elissa not joined them, they would have had one extra.

105 Now Yeshua spoke to them, saying, "You hold in your hand, not solid water, but a common rock of the Earth, in a most uncommon form, grown into the shape that you see it by the very intention of Elohim, within

the bowels of the Earth.

106 "These wands, though extraordinary, have no power of their own, but are useful tools to help you focus and magnify the Celestine Light that flows in you, to call to you the greater forces beyond and to impede and counter dark forces that may oppose you such as this terrible vortex of darkness we stand within even now."

107 At his words, everyone looked around trying to see what it was he was speaking about and each cast glances at their wand, for never had they seen anything like it, and Cephas had not even hinted that he carried them.

108 Yeshua spoke again, saying, "we are here to subdue the darkness and bring the Celestine Light that this city and the lands nearby may no longer have a shadow of death hanging over them.

109 "What I teach you today, you must teach to all other Children of Light wherever you find them, even as we have included Elissa with us this day. It matters not whether they are a part of our community or even associated with us.

110 "If you find them to be Children of Light in their hearts and the actions of their lives, share with them this knowledge as they are prepared to receive it, that they too may be a force for light against the darkness.

111 "We are standing within a dreadful vortex of darkness that has grown larger and larger, year by year, since the time of Alexander of Macedonia. It has brought a curse upon this city and land insomuch that it deadens the love and light and hope of the people. It grips their hearts with passionless disregard for life or virtue.

112 "The distance of this island city to the mainland doubled is how large a bite of the land this vortex now consumes.

113 "Let us begin by getting to know this monster. It is a ferocious whirlwind twirling rapidly, counter to the path of the Sun. We will subdue it by creating a more powerful opposing vortex of Celestine Light twirling in harmony with the Sun.

114 "There will be some among you who can see the aeon of this vortex of evil with their spiritual eyes. Others will be able to sense it and feel its putrid breath with their aura. A few may be able to both see and feel it, and some will be able to neither see it nor feel it at this time. Wherever you find yourself in your senses, you are all essential to our success.

115 "Close your eyes now and heighten your other senses. Hear the breathing of the person next to you and feel the warmth of their body.

116 "Now become aware of your personal aura, your sacred aeon. Feel it inside of you and surrounding you. Feel its movement through you and around you.

117 "Now become aware of the aura of the people on either side of you. Feel their aeon and let your aeon beat in one resonance and harmony with theirs.

118 "Now let the circle become united, one aura melded in harmony to the next and that melded in harmony to the one beside it and so on, until all within this circle are of one harmony of Celestine Light.

119 "Now that we are one light, we cannot be overcome by the darkness. Therefore, open your spiritual eyes and the fullness of your aura that you might see and feel the presence of the heartless monster whose maul we stand within. And speak out what it is you see or see not, feel or feel not."

120 As Yeshua directed, they all opened their spiritual eyes, and for some, this meant their physical eyes were open, while others kept their eyelids shut but reached out with eyes unseen to see that which physical eyes could not see.

121 And each of them opened the shields of their aura that they could feel the well of darkness they stood within.

122 Cephas was the first to speak. "I see it!" he proclaimed. "It is like the darkest cloud of the most terrible storm, circling us as fast as a whirlwind, but there is no wind," he expressed in amazement.

123 "I see it too," exclaimed Philip, "but it is translucent, not black. I can barely make it out. It is like a mirage."

124 "I neither see nor feel anything," Mattayah said with a tinge of disappointment.

125 "I cannot see it," said Yohhanan, "but opening my senses, I can feel a malevolent presence moving all around me, while I stand in a circle of golden protection."

126 One by one, they all reported that which they saw and felt or did not see or feel.

127 And there were only four besides Yeshua who both saw and felt the whirlwind of darkness, and they were Miriam, Salome, Marit, and Elissa.

128 But on this day, there was no hurt pride by the men that some of the women saw or felt what they did not, especially considering that other than Miriam, none were even Apostles. For on this day, at this moment, everyone was of one light and one heart and one thought.

129 Yeshua spoke once again, saying, "In your lives, you will encounter

vortexes of darkness of many sizes and power. Some will be smaller than a wisp of smoke from a camp fire. Others will be like this one: monsters upon the land.

130 "How large and powerful they are depends upon how dark was the deed that created them and how many years they have had to grow.

131 "Small vortexes, you can deal with individually, depending upon your natural ability and training. Larger ones require more Children of Light to be united in a circle of light.

132 "Within that circle, there will be some who are Adepts and others who are Neophytes, and this too must be taken into account, for three Adepts could subdue a vortex of the same size and power that would require one hundred Neophytes.

133 "But one Adept alone could only subdue a vortex of the same size and power that seven to nine Neophytes could subdue. Therefore, understand there is much greater power in two untied than there is in one and more still in three or twelve or more. Your individual power and intention is magnified many times by the number of you that stand shoulder to shoulder united as one.

134 "Even as you, my twelve Apostles, shall one day all be Adepts. And on that day, the power of you twelve as one shall exceed that of many thousands of novices. Therefore, take heed of my words and study and practice faithfully the secrets of Celestine Light that I share with you, that you can wield it with effectiveness in the name of Elohim.

135 "Now let us tame this beast. Each of you, take your left hand and place it on the right shoulder or waist of the person to your left. In this manner, we are all connected physically as well as aurically.

136 "Hold forth your wands with your right hand, pointing them just above our heads toward the center of our circle.

137 "Repeat now this prayer after me." And they repeated each few words immediately after he spoke them, saying, "*In the name of Elohim, we call upon the Celestine Light of Heaven to flow to us and through us, to magnify us, that we might be one with the aeon of Elohim, that we might serve our brothers and sisters and banish this darkness and free the land to live again in light. So be it!*"

138 As they spoke their last word, there was a brilliant beam of light that came forth from each of their wands, and colliding in the center of the circle, it produced a radiant flash of light that expanded quickly beyond the circle and past the confines of the room.

139 Yeshua continued to lead them, saying, "Now hold your wands pointing not to the center, but up and to the left, angled up above the head of the person to your left.

140 "Call forth your essence from within you. At the bottom of each breath, focus your essence to flow through and up your right arm, into your hand. Swirl it then for a moment, building its power still greater until your body can no more contain it, and it bursts forth from the tip of your wand.

141 "Let the power continue to flow through you and up your arm and out of your wand. Do not allow yourself to become weakened by loss of your essence, but open yourself to receive the limitless Celestine Light of Heaven and send it out through your wand.

142 "We have formed our own vortex of Celestine Light, and it swirls now in the heart of the vortex of darkness." And within the circle swirled the most amazing rainbow vortex made of innumerable scintillating points of light.

143 Yeshua continued, "Keeping your wands pointing up, in unison so that everyone's is pointing to the same degree, begin to physically swirl your wands in unison all around the circle as I do, passing over the head of each person in the circle including yourself.

144 "Let us continue this movement, increasing our speed with each revolution around the circle. Call up from within and out from the heavens for pure Celestine Light to flow to you and through you, and out your wand in unison with our brothers and sisters of the sacred circle." And the beautiful rainbow vortex expanded as they moved their wands faster and faster with each revolution around the circle.

145 "Almost complete, my brothers and sisters," Yeshua said supportively. "With one last intensity, send now a final burst of light out into this scarred land with a shout of **Elqeris**!" As Yeshua directed, so did they do.

146 When it was done, most of them fell to the ground in exhaustion, for even with the aeon they had drawn from Heaven, they had still given up much of their essence.

147 Cephas, Miriam, Yohhanan, and Yakov remained standing along with Yeshua, and he bid them to quickly go to their brothers and sisters and give them some of their essence that they might be revived, for Ashtzaph was returning in moments with soldiers.

Postscript: Vivus 66:2-3

2 When the Children of Light next met to edify one another, Yeshua spoke to them, saying, "We journeyed to Tyre not to preach, but to conquer darkness. By diminishing the darkness, we gave the people of Tyre a greater chance to find and embrace a greater portion of the light while they are in mortality.

3 To diminish darkness and bring more light to the world is one of your great purposes in life as Children of Light.

Levitation of the Twelve Apostles
Vivus: 67 3-25

(Comment: In verse 19 it mentions but does not reveal that three Words of Power were spoken to initiate the mass levitation)

3 Gathering them into a circle outside as he had done in Tyre, with Miriam on his right and Cephas on his left, with no others but Apostles present, he had them stand close and drape their arms across the back or waist of those on either side.

4 Then he instructed them further in the mysteries, saying unto them, "One of your gifts as Children of Light is to be able to float upon the air, even as a log floats upon the water, even as a bird soars on the breaths of hot air high into the sky.

5 "To accomplish this gift, you must have complete faith in Elohim and faith in yourself as a son or daughter of Elohim. And when you are joined together in a circle as we are, you must also be bound with a true love for one another with no animosities open or hidden.

6 "When you have complete faith, you have no doubt. Therefore, if there are any among you who do not have complete faith this day in either Elohim or themselves, let them step out of the circle at this time lest all be put in peril. Likewise, if any of you have issue with anyone else in this circle and do not at this moment hold a pure love for them, please step out of the circle." But none stepped out.

7 Yeshua smiled when everyone remained and told them, "I am honored to call you my brothers and to have you for my wife," he said, leaning down to give Miriam a kiss on her forehead as she looked up at him.

8 "Many of you remember the day Miriam rose a little above the ground to fetch the rock that was suspended in the air above," Yeshua began.

9 "That which we shall do today is no different than her feat then, save

your faith must be even greater than hers was upon that day. But this is easy, for united together, your faith will be greater than the faith of one and even far greater than the faith of twelve.

10 "Remember, faith is literally a tangible power, and the power of Celestine Light is multiplied, not added upon itself, with each person that is united as one within a group with purpose; even more so when it is you, my Apostles unto whom great gifts have been given.

11 "Know that it is you that shall do this, not me, for it is you that must learn to use your gifts. I am merely here to help you discover them.

12 "First, reach out with your aura and feel the aura of each and every other person in the circle. You must all be in harmony and have only pure love for one another. There can be no malice, no unforgiven grievances amongst you."

13 At this, each looked at one another and affirmed their brotherly love and that they held no grudges or grievances.

14 Yeshua continued their instruction, saying, "Because pure love is essential to the success of this gift, it is a power that can only be manifested by Children of Light, for those of the darkness do not have pure love for one another and harbor many grievances, jealousies, and hidden agendas.

15 "Though it is still dark as night, above us is a dense cloud and when the people awake, they will not find the blue sky they are accustomed to seeing most days, for it will be overcast and raining upon the land today.

16 "But above the clouds, the Sun remains, and it is there that we rise to greet the Sun. Therefore, impress that destination upon yourself. Focus upon it and leave all other thoughts behind, save rising through the clouds in the sky to the Sun above.

17 "Now to rise as one, all of our auras must be as one. Therefore, with your eyes closed, use your aura to feel the aura of the person on either side of you and harmonize and merge together until you are as one, then the person beyond them in the same manner, until all in the circle are in a harmony of one."

18 They did as Yeshua bade. When he knew that they had accomplished what he had asked, he instructed them further, "We are one. Begin to swirl our aura through our bodies in the circle. Keep it close and build its power by swirling it faster and faster in the direction of the Sun as it travels across the sky."

19 **Then he said three sacred words that cannot be written**, but only passed by the words of one Adept to another, and he told them to say these

words over and over while using their aura to sense the weight of their bodies lightening and focusing with their Xe and Ka, willing themselves up into the sky.

20 As they spoke the sacred words and did as he bade, they rose off the ground about the height of a man and as thirteen bodies holding onto one another in a circle, the circle began to spin slowly. And thus they rose up into the darkness.

21 As they rose, the sky began to lighten, and when they passed through them, the clouds were visible as a fog, although unseen to them for all still remained with their eyes closed.

22 At last, they burst through the top of the clouds and came to a stop seeming to be standing upon the clouds, and Yeshua bade them to open their eyes.

23 As they did, there were cries of wonder from almost every mouth, for they beheld a sight none had ever imagined, even a gorgeous Sun rising over a sea of clouds upon which they stood as firmly as upon the ground, though the clouds were but a dense mist.

24 There upon the cloud, in the light of the Sun, high above the Communities of Light on Lake Gennesaret, Yeshua taught them more of the mysteries of Elohim and the secrets of calling upon and using their gifts.

25 But these things cannot be written, only passed by word of mouth from one Adept to another. Thus commanded Yeshua to his Apostles, and so it is.

A Neophyte Levitates a Rock
Vivus 69:2-53

2 "Each one of you is a worker of miracles, for as Children of Light, it is your blessing to be able to call upon the greater Celestine Light of Elohim as you have needs, whatever those may be, provided you are seeking only that which is righteous and needful and not for riches or acclaim of the world.

3 "Yet you could live your entire life and never be the conduit through which a miracle flows, unless you understand the principles upon which the powers of Celestine Light bring wonder upon the Earth."

4 Reaching down, he grabbed a fist-size stone and threw it high over his head and above the lake. Turning toward the lake and extending his

arm, he pointed his right forefinger at the stone just as it reached its apex and commanded, "*Kel Arz!*" and the rock remained suspended in the air.

5 Turning to look over his left shoulder at the Children of Light, he said unto them, "You see a rock that does not fall, and because every rock you have ever seen thrown into the air always falls, you think that you now see a miracle or magick.

6 "But verily, I say unto you: There are no miracles or magick. These are merely what the ignorant call events they do not understand, which seem to violate all that they hold as natural and normal.

7 "In truth, every miracle or act of magick from a healing to a rock floating in air is but the manifestation of a natural law created by Elohim that is unknown to the world, but given to be known and understood by Children of Light of uprightness and virtue."

8 Then he quickly sliced his arm through the air, and bringing his hand to his side, he turned again to face the Children of Light, even as the rock plummeted and fell into the lake behind him with a loud splash.

9 He continued to instruct them, saying, "The rock remained suspended in the air, not because Elohim made a great miracle, but because I understand all of the natural laws created by the Elohim and called upon the aeon of those I needed to cause this rock not to fall.

10 "And what are these natural laws to be known by the Children of Light but mysteries to the world? They begin with faith and love. These two essences, which you cannot hold in your hand, are some of the essential attributes needed to affect the physical world, including suspending rocks in the air.

11 "This is incomprehensible to the people of the world. They understand how one physical action can create another, such as when you hit a tree sufficient times with an axe, it is felled. But it would seem the greatest mystery of magick were the same tree to be felled without anything physically touching it, but merely by the unseen powers of faith, love, passion, and focus, harmonized with the knowledge of how to use the unseen aeons of Celestine Light.

12 "Understand that it is by absolute faith in our Mother and Father in Heaven, whom we cannot see, that we can call the unseen forces of the Celestine Light to manifest that which is seen.

13 "It is because of my love for you and desire to see you grow in the Celestine Light that the aeons activated by my faith come to me when I bid them.

14 "I pointed my finger at the rock just as it reached its apex, when it was neither propelled to continue rising higher, nor compelled to descend rapidly downward into the lake. This was the easiest moment to have effect upon it.

15 "With my eyes steadfastly upon the stone high in the air, I extended my arm and pointed my finger at it that the energies of Heaven flowing through me would be exactly focused and could have a most sure effect.

16 "Understand then that undiluted and undistracted focus upon your desire is also imperative to your success. But no less than this is, you must also have a passion to see your desire accomplished.

17 "By extending your arm and your finger, you are channeling all of the necessary aeons through a long conduit and the single small point of your fingertip. As the powers of Celestine Light swirl inside of you and then travel through your arm, they compress and increase their strength.

18 "As the aeon shoots from your fingertip, it is both highly focused and of greater power because of the focus through a narrow channel. This effect can be even further enhanced by holding another object that is both long and slender, coming to a point, and intrinsically holding Celestine aeons, such as a crystal, a spiral shell, or a specifically fashioned wand of wood and gems."

19 Yeshua then beckoned a young man of about fourteen years to come to him, and a youth of humble and noble visage stepped forward from among the Children of Light.

20 "You are the son of Daoud and Thara, who recently came to us from the wilderness beyond Bahr Lut?"

21 The young man nodded his head affirmatively and said, "Yes, most revered teacher and light of lights. I am Galal. My father saw a vision in the night as he slept, and so real it was he thought he was awake.

22 "He saw these communities upon the lake and saw you clearly although he had never in life even heard your name.

23 "He saw a pillar of light pierce dark clouds in the sky and fall upon you as you walked in these communities, and a voice came upon his mind, saying, 'Behold the light of the world.' The very next day, our family departed from our brethren and have lived now among you for these past two moons."

24 "And we are happy that you are among us," Yeshua said unto him. "Truly, you and your parents and your brothers and sisters are Children of Light and one with us. What the world would separate, Elohim has

brought together."

25 Yeshua looked upon him squarely and asked, "Before you came among us, you were raised to believe in a God that is different than we know. For Elohim of the Children of Light is different than the imagined God of the Hebrews or the Egyptians or any other that men do worship and venerate.

26 "Having lived among us now for a short time and having learned somewhat of our ways, have you through your prayers and in your heart and mind come to a greater understanding?"

27 Galal nodded affirmatively and said unto Yeshua, "I have a witness in my heart and head that cannot be denied, nor would I dare even on pain of death. My witness is that I have a divine Father and Mother in Heaven and that I am their son of spirit.

28 "So too have I a noble brother of spirit, who is their son of the flesh. And he ever watches over me as an elder brother should. And through them, we call the Elohim, by our efforts and virtue, all good things come and all things are possible."

29 Yeshua looked upon the Children of Light before him and said unto them, "Verily, no greater testimony of the Celestine Light could be given than this. Galal may be young in years, but his soul resonates with the wisdom of Heaven."

30 Then Yeshua bent down and whispered into Galal's ear, saying, "Do as I shall direct, hold your faith true and unwavering, and do not be weakened in your conviction or focus if you do not succeed on your first attempt, for he who perseveres with faith, focus, passion, and love shall succeed."

31 Then rising, he again addressed the Children of Light, saying, "I have explained to you how to hold a stone in the air. Size is important, and the larger or heavier an object is, the greater aeon is required to hold it or move it.

32 The words you heard me command, "*Kel Arz!*" are not found among the languages of men, but are words of power from the Celestine language of the Elohim. Spoken by unbelievers, they are merely empty words, but spoken by a Child of Light, for a purpose of righteousness, with faith, love, passion, and focus, they call upon a great aeon of the heavens, which overcomes the lesser aeon by which all things fall to Earth."

33 Turning to Galal, he reached down and picked up a stone, and instructed, "As you saw me do, so do you now."

34 Galal's eyes went wide in astonishment, but quickly became peaceful and resolute as he took the stone from Yeshua and turned to face the lake. For a moment, he remained silent with his head bowed in contemplation and perhaps a silent prayer.

35 Then he threw the stone high into the air, and as it reached its apex, he extended his arm and, pointing his finger, yelled out, *"Kel Arz!"* However, the rock did not hesitate or remain in the air, but ignoring his words and intent, it fell quickly back into the lake with a high splash.

36 Galal looked back to Yeshua with some embarrassment upon his face, but Yeshua smiled at him and patted him on the back, assuring him that he did well.

37 He then reached upon the ground and picked up a fairly straight stick about the length of his arm and snapped a third of it off including the unbroken tip and handed it to Galal, saying, "Hold this stick in your right hand and point it instead of your finger. And remember to have a passion for your desire." Then he threw another stone into the sky, and once more Galal waited until it was at its apex then extended his arm and pointing at the rock with the stick he held, he commanded, *"Kel Arz!"*

36 For the barest moment, it seemed that the rock lingered for an extra heartbeat at its apex; then it too fell into the lake.

39 Galal looked back to Yeshua, and Yeshua took the stick from his hand. Then reaching inside his clothing, he pulled out another stick about the same length as the first, only this one was perfectly straight and tapered to a distinct but rounded point with a delicate spiral pattern finely cut into it, beginning at its base and rising to its tip. Its wood was very dark and unfamiliar to Galal as he took it and rolled it in his hands after Yeshua handed to him.

40 Without further instructions or words, Yeshua reached down and picked up another stone and threw it high into the air above the lake.

41 Once more, Galal waited until the rock reached its apex, then extending his arm and pointing the fine spiraled stick, he commanded, *"Kel Arz!"* and this time, the rock remained undeniably suspended in the air.

42 As it did, there was an audible gasp from those who were watching and Galal moved his eyes for a moment to look at the crowd, and when he did, the rock immediately fell into the lake.

43 Again Yeshua smiled at him but did not speak. But he did hold out his hand by way of asking for Galal to return the spiral stick to him. But

in its stead, he took out another item from within his clothing and handed it to Galal.

44 This new item was also a like a stick, but one such as neither Galal nor any but the Apostles had ever seen, for it was heavy and made of clear crystal, having also been finely worked with a spiral pattern. On its base was a rounded cap of deep-blue Lapis spider webbed with golden lines and held to the crystal wand by a band of gold.

45 Turning to the Children of Light, Yeshua said unto them, "When you have learned to harness all of the aeons Elohim has blessed the Children of Light to know, you will have no need for sticks or wands of crystal to aid you in accomplishing that which you desire.

46 "But until that day, there are tools upon the Earth that can magnify your abilities because they readily call to them the aeons you seek and further amplify the power of Celestine Light that flows through you.

47 "You have seen what was manifested by the finger of Galal and when he held a simple stick and then a wand of wood fashioned to serve the Children of Light. Now he holds a wand of crystal put upon the Earth by Elohim and spiral cut and inlaid with gold and Lapiz by my own hands. It resonates with the powers of Heaven and beckons still greater aeons to aid young Galal in his quest. See now the final difference."

48 Once more he threw a stone into the air, and once more Galal thrust his arm upward and pointed the crystal wand at the rock as it reached its apex, commanding in a loud voice, "*Kel Arz!*" This time, the stone remained in the sky and did not fall back to Earth.

49 As Galal continued to focus his eyes and thoughts upon the stone, Yeshua spoke to him, saying, "You now are one with the stone. It is merely an extension of you. Like your own hand, it moves where you guide it and will it to move. Therefore, continuing to point the wand of crystal and keeping your focus, move the stone some distance to the right."

50 As Yeshua bid so Galal did, and there were more gasps from the spectators as the stone moved the length of a fishing boat to the right.

51 "Now make the stone begin to dance," Yeshua bade. "Move it up and down and all around."

52 Again, as Yeshua bade so Galal did. And the stone moved through the air following exactly as he moved his arm in a figure-eight pattern. Then he brought the stone down to a point that it nearly touched the water, and he held it there.

53 Yeshua put his right hand upon his head, saying, "Well done, good

brother of light. You may release the stone now." As he spoke, Galal quickly pulled the wand away from the lake and handed it to Yeshua, and the stone quietly dropped into the water.

Miriam Mesmorizes Roman Soliders
Vivus 71:6-15

6 Thus it was on this day that while over sixty of the Children of Light came to the springs to soak and meditate, six soldiers of Herod barred their way and ordered them to depart immediately as judges of the Greater Sanhedrin of Jerusalem had just arrived in Tiberias and were coming to the springs within the hour to bathe in privacy.

7 Without thought of protest or complaint, almost everyone nodded their heads and made to comply, as no one desired unwanted attention from either Herod's soldiers or the Sanhedrin.

8 But Miriam, who was standing with Yeshua, Salome, Martha, Miryam, and their children, was incensed, for they had barely arrived after a long walk on a hot day. Turning to Yeshua, she asked, "Must we always be meek as sheep, beloved?"

9 He answered her, saying, "Today is as good a day as any to begin our inevitable confrontations with the Sanhedrin. If it is in your power to make it so without harm to any of the Children of Light, let it be so Miriam."

10 With Yeshua's approval, Miriam looked steadfastly upon the soldiers of Herod and pulled from beneath her garment the rainbow crystal that hung from a chain on her neck.

11 She removed the chain from her neck, and holding the crystal and chain in her right hand, she stepped in front of the soldiers, and pointing the point of the crystal at them, she moved it in three circuits in a wide figure-eight motion, while quietly speaking words that none could hear.

12 "What is that you are doing, witch?" shouted one of the soldiers. "Stop this instant if you value your life."

13 But she did not stop, and the man who spoke and another made to take a step toward her but stopped in mid-stride as she transferred the crystal to her left hand in a very fluid movement, and held up her right hand as she had on the river Qishon, with the palm upward and her fingers splayed, and said, "*Ollinaris*," in a firm but quiet voice.

14 Suddenly, all of the soldiers seemed to fall into a stupor. They gazed

ahead but did not see. That lasted but a few seconds, and then the soldier that had confronted Miriam looked at her and said amiably, "You may pass, and we shall protect your privacy."

15 Thus did all of the Children of Light who were present pass by the soldiers of Herod and into the baths of Tiberius. Many looked at the soldiers with incredulity as they passed, wondering what had occurred, for few had seen what Miriam had done. But the soldiers regarded them not at all and stared straight ahead as they passed by.

Yeshua and Miriam Restore Life to a Wooden Gate
Vivus 71:73-96

73 "I have answered you fully," Yeshua replied. "But only the humble hear and understand my words." Without another word, Yeshua turned and walked away from the vice-chief justice and toward the wooden gate that was the entrance to the baths. Seeing him approach the guards of Herod stepped aside.

74 As Yeshua departed in silence, Abraham ben Obias turned to his fellow Sanhedrin and gloated, "Certainly, put that simpleton in his place." A hearty round of laughter came from the Sanhedrin in agreement.

75 As Yeshua turned toward the door, he called out to Miriam in his mind, beckoning her to come with him to the entry gate and explained to her his intention as they took the few steps.

76 Without drawing notice, the milling Apostles blocked the view of Yeshua and Miriam, who had disappeared behind them, from everyone on the street.

77 Coming to the gate, Yeshua put his right hand upon it and Miriam her left, and they looked at each other with subtle, knowing smiles and together said in quiet voices, "Elxpedia." After only a few seconds, they removed their hands and walked away with the Apostles, accompanied by taunts from some in the crowd.

78 As they were still laughing and commenting about the encounter with Yeshua, it was a few minutes before the Sanhedrin approached the gate to enter the baths. When they did, they discovered it would not open.

79 The vice-chief justice looked at the guards of Herod and commanded them to open the gate, but even with the two pounding against it with their shoulders and all their weight, it would not budge.

80 "What can possibly be the problem with a simple gate?" demanded

Abraham ben Obias.

81 The guards could not answer, for the gate had no locking mechanism and only hung loosely in the portal, although it seemed to have swollen until it occupied all of the space with no light escaping around the edges from the side beyond.

82 Seeing the continued commotion, the Roman soldiers, who had been observing the events from the far street corner, came up to the gate to discover what was causing the continuing disturbance. But they too could not open the gate.

83 The commander gave an order to one of the soldiers, and he departed, but soon returned with an axe and commenced to take mighty swings into the wooden door.

84 Meanwhile, Yeshua and the Apostles had met up with the last of the Children of Light who had departed from the baths, and Salome was among them.

85 She came up and embraced Miriam and said unto her, "We stayed longer than most of the others, for when you did not return, they began to worry and departed with all the children by the lake gate. I was worried for you also, as we could hear the voices of angry men, and we saw the funnel cloud of dust and heard the dreadful screaming of we know not what."

86 Miriam walked with her, holding her hand, and told her all that had transpired with Yeshua, and the Sanhedrin and Salome was astounded. "And what of the gate?" she asked. "How did you stop it from opening? And why did Yeshua ask you to come with him?"

87 Miriam answered her with a wry smile, saying, "We merely rejoined in life that which Heavenly Father and Heavenly Mother had created, but man had torn asunder. Where boards had been, a tree became.

88 "Yeshua could have accomplished it alone, but in his love asked me to help; and in truth, the spark of life most easily comes with the union of male and female."

89 Back at the gate, the Roman soldiers had taken huge chunks out of the wood with the axe so much so that the head of the axe now disappeared beneath the wood with every chop. Yet still the gate did not open. The commander looked to Herod's soldiers and demanded, "How thick is this infernal gate? I passed through it just yesterday and remember it as nothing more than rough hewn boards."

90 "And so it was," answered one of Herod's guards. "I know not what

has become of it, save the Galilean prophet touched it just before he departed, along with a woman."

91 "Look!" exclaimed one of the Sanhedrin, pointing to the door. "It lives!"

92 Everyone looked to where he was pointing, and there was a sprout of green leaves coming out of the wooden gate. More were quickly noticed shooting out of the wood in several places.

93 "This is impossible!" exclaimed the commander of the Romans. He ordered his men to dig down into the ground beneath the gate.

94 "The gate continues beneath the ground!" shouted one of the digging soldiers incredulously. "By Jupiter! This is a tree, and these are its roots!"

95 Seeing what his eyes could scarcely believe, Abraham ben Obias looked with some apprehension in the direction Yeshua had departed, and one of his fellow judges standing beside him asked, "What manner of man can turn a gate of boards into a living tree? Is not life the domain of God? Surely, magick like this has never been seen in Israel."

96 Abraham continued to look with vacant puzzlement out into the distance and answered almost in a whisper, "Surely not."

Miriam Stops a Stoning and Blinds the Assailants
Vivus 84:7-46

(Comment: There are so many good lessons in this story that I included it in entirety rather than just excerpt the part where Miriam uses a Word of Power. Those familiar with the Christian New Testament might recognize this as a much fuller and very different account of a brief mention in the NT of "He who is without sin, let him cast the first stone.)

7 In yet one more attempt to discredit Yeshua in the eyes of the common people and prove that he disobeyed well known and widely accepted laws, the Pharisees found him with his small entourage resting under a tree in a plaza and brought a woman accused of adultery before him. A crowd of perhaps forty men followed them.

8 The woman was cloaked completely in black, including a hood covering her head with only a woven mesh for her to see out of and breathe near her eyes and nose. She was whimpering in fear as she was thrust prone onto the ground at Yeshua's feet.

9 "Rabbi, this woman has been charged with adultery," one of the Pharisees spat out in contempt, looking at Yeshua. "Two honorable men

have born witness against her and the man with whom she committed her sin has also confessed. They are standing there among these good men of Israel," he said, pointing into the crowd.

10 The Pharisee turned and looked out upon the gathered men declaring, "By the laws of God she must be punished with stoning. If God wills it, she will die. If not, so be it. We are merely the hands of God to execute his will."

11 Speaking to the crowd, the Pharisee called out, "Who here will cast a stone and be a servant of the Almighty?" As if they had never heard a word of the teachings of Yeshua there was a chorus of 'ayes' and many men, including her accusers hastily searched the surrounding ground and picked up rocks, some of them larger than a fist.

12 The Pharisee looked at Yeshua smugly, saying, "Rabbi, it is you who should give the command for her to be stoned. By this we will all know that in truth you uphold and support the laws of Israel and God."

13 Seeing this spectacle, the ordeal of the woman, the willingness of the mob to so easily be swayed to violence, and the Pharisees rude and despicable behavior, Miriam began to step forward to confront them with righteous anger and perhaps more, but Yeshua grasped her garment and held her back.

14 Holding her hand he stepped with her in front of the woman upon the ground, standing between the accused woman and the Pharisees and the crowd of men.

15 Yeshua shook his head and said unto them, "How easily you forget all that you have heard me teach as I have traveled through your towns. Do you think that my miracles come from God but not my teachings? I ask you in the name of Elohim, the God of fairness, why is the woman put to death while the man who sinned with her is merely given a few lashes and then given a stone with which to injure her grievously or contribute to her death?

16 "Was it the woman who lusted for the man and convinced him to commit adultery, or the man who lusted for the woman and convinced her? All of you men already know the answer in your heart, for it is in men that lust leads to stupidity and sweet words of false love to entice women of virtue into abasement."

17 Looking at the Pharisees, Yeshua scolded them, saying, "Woe unto you Pharisees for trying to spring a trap of the law upon me. Have you not already heard me say that I have not come to support the law that is

unjust, but to overthrow it and crush it beneath my feet?"

18 Turning again to the gathered men, Yeshua said unto them, "Are you the just judging the unjust, or are you the unjust seeking to condemn another when your own house is a cesspool? Alright brave men of Israel. You seek the justice of your law by your own hands? Then let he who is without sin among you be the only ones to cast a stone, else you are the unrighteous judging the unrighteous, and where is the justice in that?"

19 Hearing his words a few men dropped their stones, but most held onto them with lethal intent and it was plain that for most of the men, his words had fallen on deaf ears, for from among the crowd came shouts of, "Death to the adulteress!" "Serve God!" "Uphold the laws of Israel!"

20 Yeshua breathed a deep sigh of disappointment and spoke to Miriam in his mind, saying, "These men are blind to the truth, let them be blind for a short time to life and perhaps then they will give it greater value. I leave it to you Miriam to protect this woman and teach these men the majesty of the Celestine Light in a way that they will never desire to repeat this event. Use the gifts you have been given, in the fullness you have learned so well."

21 "As you wish my Lord," she acknowledged in their unspoken communication. "Very happily it shall be."

22 Even in that short silent exchange between Yeshua and Miriam, a group of over a dozen men with one or more stones in their hands had formed a half circle close about Yeshua, Miriam and the women in black, who was now sitting upon the ground, still whimpering in fear. The Pharisees had faded back behind the men intent upon stoning the woman, and a larger group of onlookers had gathered behind the original group of men waiting to see what would transpire.

23 Miriam stepped away from Yeshua and took a step forward toward the threatening men. Yeshua stood immediately beside the woman in black. Salome and his three Apostles stood a pace or so behind her.

24 "Good men of Israel. Drop your stones and move away, before you reap in pain what you sow in foolishness," Miriam commanded. "You will not stone this woman today or any other. You are merely being used by the Pharisees. They think you are ignorant louts that they can manipulate to hurt Yeshua of Nazareth. Are you going to prove them right or show them you are men touched by the light?"

25 "Ha!" Exclaimed one of the Pharisees standing behind the men holding stones. "Does the scandalously uncovered wife of the Rabbi now

speak for her husband, because her husband listens more to his brazen, disobedient wife than to God?

26 "What more proof of blasphemy than this—that any woman, let alone one so shamelessly unclothed, would be so insolent to command men, and her husband, the good Rabbi, would simply stand idly by and not rebuke her?"

27 There were many grumblings of agreement in the crowd at the words of the Pharisee, both among the men with stones and in the multitude that stood back observing the events.

28 Hearing this, Yeshua spoke to the Pharisee, saying, "Rather than rebuke my wife, I am the one that has always asked her to dress more in the manner of the Greeks, to not hide the beauty that Elohim created.

29 "It is I who has also asked her to speak. The blasphemy against Elohim is not in a woman showing her beauty, or speaking, or commanding men, but in your laws which condemn such. Until you realize women are your equals, not your property; your co-creators in both this life and the next; you will never know God or taste the fruits of the life to come."

30 "Stone her!" Yelled out someone from the crowd. "Stone her!" More voices repeated.

31 "Move aside Rabbi," ordered the Pharisee. "And your wife and disciples as well. This crowd has heard your words and they have heard mine. They have seen your actions and judged them to not be in keeping with the teachings of God. You are not judged to be stoned this day, but this woman is, and her time has come to receive the wrath of God for her iniquity. Stand aside at this moment lest you and your wives and disciples all suffer her fate by proximity."

32 But among the Celestines—Yeshua, Miriam, Salome and the three Apostles, not one moved or spoke in response to the admonition of the Pharisee. They all stood resolute, courageously facing the ring of the men with stones.

33 "Stone her!" Someone yelled once again. At this latest call the men holding the rocks quickly raised up their arms to cast their stones, even as more men in the crowd behind picked up stones from the ground so they too could participate in the judgment.

34 Miriam's eyes narrowed as she saw the men raising their arms with lethal intent. As their arms whipped forward slinging their missiles she uttered a single Celestine word of power, "*Lakadonz!*" Ere the word left her lips the hurtling rocks instantly disintegrated into sand in midair and

fell harmlessly to the ground.

35 Immediately after uttering the word of power, in a rapid sweeping motion, Miriam put her hands in the prayer position across her chest than quickly raised them high, opening her palms and spreading out her fingers. At her beckoning, the fallen sand from the former stones was joined by a rapidly forming whirlwind of sand and dust from the ground.

36 So thick was the swirling mass that the entire multitude quickly disappeared behind the funnel cloud. In its calm core the woman in black stood up in amazement looking at the wall of fury just beyond her touch, while in the peaceful center she remained with Yeshua, Miriam, Salome and the three Apostles.

37 After just a minute or two the whirlwind settled and vanished. A haze of dust remained hanging in the air. Many of the crowd had hurriedly dispersed to escape the biting sand and dust, but many still remained including the Pharisees and each of the would-be assailants. But every man who had held a stone now held their eyes moaning in misery and stumbling and falling in blindness.

38 One by one friends and family of the stricken men came to them and led them away. The Pharisees also gathered together disheveled and confused and departed without saying another word.

39 When all of her adversaries were gone Yeshua turned to the woman in black, saying, "Where are your accusers who would condemn you?"

40 The women shrugged and answered meekly, "I know not sir, they are not here."

41 "Nor are there any among us that would condemn or judge you," Yeshua assured her.

42 "You save the unworthy good sir," the woman said, bowing her head deeply with a long sigh and a burst of crying. "I am guilty of that of which I have been accused. I hate myself for what I have done, but it does not change that which has transpired."

43 Yeshua put his hand gently on the top of her head, "But your true and remorseful repentance has changed you. And it has changed your present and your future as you continue to walk in the light from this day forth.

44 "Because of your repentance, the Elohim do not condemn you for your sin, nor even remember it any more. I know the depth of your sorrow for all that has transpired. Go your way and sin like this no more. Prove yourself worthy of the life you have been given again this day. Live it in the

light that all who truly know you will praise you and your virtues."

45 The woman then departed, thanking Yeshua and Miriam profusely and two of the Apostles went with her to see her safely to her home. Watching them leave Salome put her hand gently upon Miriam's shoulder and asked, "What of the men who became blind in the sandstorm? Will their sight return?"

46 "Yes," Miriam assured her. "Yeshua only meant for them to have a lesson equal to their folly. It is important when true justice issues from the Celestine Light of Elohim that it is in actuality just and fair. Neither too harsh nor too lenient from the punishment that is warranted."

Salome Opens a Portal to Another Dimension
Vivus 95:12-35

(Comment: This is another instance where the actual Word of Power that was spoken is not written, but is specifically mentioned.)

12 Not far from the river bank, Yeshua took a stick and drew a diagram in the dirt at their feet and told them, "To pass through the gateway into the shadow Earth at a time other than its usual and accustomed opening, you must draw this diagram vertically in the air at the place of the gateway, with a consecrated wooden wand or rainbow crystal, as if you were drawing on a door of wood at the entrance of a building."

13. Yeshua *spoke again a Celestine word of power* unto them and cautioned, "I command you once again to never reveal this word or the diagram that I shall now show unto you, to any, save those who are Adepts among the Celestine Children of Light."

14. "After you have drawn the diagram, speak the word of power I have given you, and the gateway shall be revealed and open to you. It is that simple, at least if you also have all of the other qualities of a higher adept of the Celestine Light.

15 "When I am not with you, never pass through the gateway without a consecrated rainbow crystal to amplify the light of Elohim upon you, lest harm come upon you while you are in one of the worlds of the lower kingdoms.

16 "A consecrated rainbow crystal coupled with your great faith, will always allow you to return to your Earth at the instant you merely think for it to be so. There is nothing else you need do if you have correctly imbued the sacred object with the Celestine Light of Elohim and a connection to

this Earth as you have been taught."

17 Yeshua turned to Salome. "It is fitting that the one among you who could first see the gateway should be the one who opens the door."

18 He looked to Miriam who was standing beside him and asked, "May Salome use your consecrated crystal to open the gateway?"

19 "Of course my Lord," Miriam answered. She reached inside her garments and lifted a gold chain from around her neck. Dangling from it was a clear crystal about the size of her index finger that radiated the colors of the rainbow.

20 She handed the crystal to Salome who turned to Yeshua waiting for his instructions.

21 "Curl the golden chain in the palm of your hand and hold the point of the crystal parallel to the ground pointing away from you", he instructed.

22 He continued, "turn slowly now in a circle with the thought in your mind to discover the location of the nearest gateway."

23 Salome did as Yeshua told her, and as she was almost at the point of completing a circle she suddenly lurched forward as if an invisible person had grabbed her by her outstretched arm and pulled her toward them.

24 "Oh my!" she exclaimed. "I am being physically and strongly pulled forward. I must indeed resist if I am to remain rooted and not step forward."

25 "Consecrated wands of wood and rainbow crystals act as tools of resonance when you have imbued them with the energy you seek," Yeshua explained. "As you are all Celestine Adepts you can do this with simply a thought.

26 "Once imbued with righteous purpose they sing in harmony with that which you seek. When you are far from it, they will merely whisper and the pull of direction will be ever so slight.

27 "But when you are upon the item, place or person that you seek, the pull will be so strong that you will have no doubt that you have arrived.

28 "Step forward into that which pulls you until something changes." Yeshua instructed Salome.

29 She did as he bade and moved forward four steps with her arm outstretched, pointing the crystal before her. Suddenly she stopped and turning to Yeshua, said, "I am no longer being pulled. The crystal is radiating heat, but no longer is an invisible hand pulling me forward."

30 "You are no longer being pulled because you have arrived at your destination." Yeshua affirmed.

31 "Now take the tip of the crystal and draw the diagram I have shown

you, in the same size that I drew, vertically in the air before you. When you are finished say the Celestine word of power that I gave to you. In a whisper or a roar it is the same, as long as you speak the word aloud."

32 Once more Salome did as Yeshua bade her, and as soon as she spoke the word of power the shimmering, blue spiral gateway opened directly in front of her, taller by a head than she, and the width of her arms if they were extended to either side.

33 Miriam came to Yeshua on his right side and slipped her arm through his and held close to him. Yeshua stepped forward and Salome came to his other side and also put her arm through his and held close to him.

34 Together they stepped forward into the turning blue spiral light and disappeared.

Miriam Creates a Bubble of Warmth and Light on a Cold World
Vivus 95:39-48

39 When they arrived on the other side of the gateway their enthusiasm was quickly dampened by the dark and foreboding world in which they found themselves.

40 Yeshua, Miriam and Salome stood facing them as they came through the portal. As the last Apostle came through they all looked around in silence at the strange world to which they had come.

41 In mere moments they were all shivering and holding their arms across their chests or rubbing their hands together in a feeble attempt to stay warm. "This is the coldest place I have ever been." Philip said through chattering teeth.

42 "I thought it was night when we first stepped into this world." Shim'on said as he covered his face with his hands and then pointed with one at the sky, saying, "But there is the puny sun, I think, low on the horizon and barely seen through the thick, dark clouds that lay even upon the ground."

43 Miriam turned to Salome and asked for the crystal on the gold chain she had given to her to open the portal.

44 When she had it in hand, she pointed the crystal toward the ground and then drew her outstretched arm in an arch over the grouped Apostles, ending the arch on the far side of the ground from where she had begun, then spoke a single Celestine word of power, "*Saxteris*."

45 Immediately a bubble of warm light was created surrounding the

Apostles, and Yeshua, Miriam and Salome stepped into it with them.

46 "What wonder is this?" asked Toma, as he stood with open arms and palms up basking in the new found warmth of their sanctuary from the cold.

47 "Can you teach me to do that Miriam?" asked Yohanan with child-like enthusiasm. "Or is it something only you can do because of your calling as an angel?

48 "This is a blessing given to any virtuous Child of Light to do as they are prepared in heart and mind, certainly any that are Adepts", she answered calmly. "I can teach you the method Yohanan, but only the faith of a child, singular focus, and the harmony of oneness will manifest it for you."

Cephas Opens a Dimensional Portal
Vivus 95:43-46

43 Yeshua asked Miriam to give her crystal to anyone she chose that they could open the portal. She handed it gently to Cephas who was standing near her.

44 Yeshua pointed to the spot where they had come through, saying, "Draw the diagram in the air as you saw Salome do and say the *Celestine word of power* that I gave to you."

45 Cephas did as Yeshua bade and the shimmering blue gateway immediately opened before them spinning in a slow spiral.

46 Cephas turned back to look at Yeshua and he nodded for him to proceed, so he stepped through the portal and was followed by all of the Apostles, Salome, Miriam and lastly, Yeshua.

Yuda the Younger Opens a Dimensional Portal
Vivus 98:32

32 Yuda smiled with almost childlike enthusiasm. After looking to Yeshua and getting a nod of approval, he went over to the wall and using the tip of his wand he drew the Celestine diagram to open the portal and uttered the *Celestine word of power*. Immediately the shimmering, unearthly blue spiral light appeared, and the portal opened before them in the wall the height and breadth of a man. The wall became opaquely translucent at that spot, and though it could dimly be seen, there was a

land that was far different than the land that was usually on the other side of the wall.

Yeshua Explains Celestine Gifts of Power
Vivus 98:63-70

63 Yeshua answered, saying, "As I have said before, where much has been given for you to know, much is expected for you to do. You have received great gifts of Celestine Light that you may accomplish great things. When you have a light you do not hide it under a basket; and you are the lights of the world.

64 Tomorrow is the day that the weak will become strong and the ignorant enlightened. But today is the day that the strong recognize their strength. Today is the day that you discover who you really are."

65 Cephas took a step forward and holding his hands spread in front of him he lifted them up and down, saying, "We have all been practicing, a little here and a little there with our gifts." He cupped his hands closely together with his palms up, "but it is only this little bit that we have actually mastered.

66 I think I am further along than most, but even so, I would still prefer a sharp sword or a stout staff to defend myself against attackers until you have taught us more in the ways to call forth our gifts of Celestine Light with power and focused direction, and we have had more time to practice using what knowledge we gain."

67 Yeshua smiled slightly as he answered Cephas, saying, "Swords may help you against brigands on your Earth, but here, they would be as useless against your foes as throwing an ant at an armored Roman soldier. Only your gifts will save you."

68 Looking around at all of them, he elaborated, "There are some things that need to be taught, such as Celestine words of power that call in certain specific forces of the Celestine Light, but these things you have already learned in our days together.

69 What remains is simply the need for total faith in Elohim, in yourself, and in the gifts that you know you have. That and a love for your brethren and a passion to succeed using your gifts. Remember, even if they have yet to be seen, I have told you that you have these gifts, therefore you know that it is so.

70 You have heard me teach often that with faith nothing is impossible

to you. If you believe in me, you must also believe in yourselves, else you deny your belief in me.

Miriam Neutralizes a Threat to Her Brother
Vivus 98:98-104

98 "Our bodies are not our own," Cephas called out to Yeshua in his mind. "We are possessed of demons and are being compelled against our will. Help us!"

99 Miriam heard the voice of Salome calling to her in her mind, pleading, "Miriam, please help me! My body moves even though I command it to stay. I try to resist and there is terrible pain through all of my body. It is unbearable! Please help me!"

100 Hearing Salome in agony Miriam looked to Yeshua, but knowing her thoughts to rescue Salome, he shook his head and said unto her in her mind, "We must love them enough to let them fight their own fight and find themselves and their own power."

101 "But this is so strange to them, my Lord," Miriam spoke aloud to him. "Their senses and their minds are overwhelmed, so much so they cannot even line up their thoughts to consider how to use their gifts to resist. Most of them are so confused they cannot even speak to us in their minds."

102 Yeshua nodded in agreement and answered, "Nevertheless, we must give them time to discover themselves. They will be in pain, but will not be killed, even if they resist."

103 He then pointed to Lazarus walking away and said, "But see to the safety of your brother, for he has not been given the gifts of the Apostles and goes happily as a lamb to the slaughter without understanding the consequences or means to prevent them."

104 Miriam nodded her head in agreement and forcefully thrust each hand skyward with fingers splayed, each pointing toward one of the orbs hovering over them. She closed her eyes and *uttered a single Celestine word of power* and immediately both orbs dropped to the ground with clanging metallic thunks and rolled down the slope to come to rest at its base.

Miriam Opens an Orb
Vivus 98:146:-153

146 Yeshua again addressed the Apostles, saying, "You may now freely touch the orbs. They will not harm you as they did Lazarus when he touched one on the ground. I will tell you that they are not life, but creations of the people who live here. But be gentle with them, for they contain a surprise within that must not be damaged."

147 "A surprise?" Mused Amram. "Perhaps some food, for I am hungry after all of this unfamiliar Xe and Ka exertion."

148 "We shall see," Yeshua replied pointing toward the orb laying on the ground nearest Amram. "Let us open one that you may discover its contents."

149 Amram went over and hefted the orb, saying, "It is very light. I do not think there is any food inside of it."

150 He shook it gently, observing, "I do not hear anything rattling around inside. Nor can I see any way to get into it other than punching a hole with something sharp, for there are no seams."

151 He knocked on it with his knuckles producing a faint empty echo. "I think it is hollow, but we will have to make a hole in it to see inside."

152 "I think not," Yeshua responded. "There is a way in, but Miriam will need to open it. Surely, each of you could accomplish it, but until you see her do it, you would spend too long of a time trying to fathom it and we have much still to do."

153 Hearing Yeshua's words, Miriam went over to the orb next to Amram. She placed a hand on opposite sides of the orb, then said the Celestine word of power, *Ezavant*. Immediately a seam appeared around the circumference of the orb and one half of it slid back inside the other half, revealing a small unmoving figure, dressed in resplendent clothing and accouterments, reclining on its back in a tiny chair.

A Circle of Power Invokes a Veil of Illusion and Teleportation
Vivus 100:12:28

12 When the children all had rejoined the circle with their crystal wands in hand, Yeshua spoke again to everyone, saying, "Close your eyes now so you are not distracted by anything around you. Remember friends

and strangers you have encountered in your life that were Children of Light, even those who may not have known they were, but whose lives of goodness, love and stewardship, left no doubt.

13 "Remember your wives and children who may not be here now and how much you love them and wish they were here in spirit and so shall they be.

14 "Those of you who have walked with me upon the Earth as I have shared the teachings of the Elohim, remember the special people whom we have encountered over the years. See them clearly in your mind, hear their voice, look into their eyes.

15 "Now each person, man, woman and child, holding your wand in your right hand, point it toward the center of the circle and place your left hand on the shoulder or around the waist of the person to your left. In this, stand closely together with each of the people beside you so that your shoulders or sides are also touching.

16 "You that are many are now becoming one in the light and the light shall be in you and outside of you, all around you, and multiplied many, many times more than your numbers.

17 "Reflect upon your love for the person to your right and to your left and for all the other brothers and sisters of the Celestine Light that are one in this circle with you.

18 "Remember your faith. Feel it welling up deep inside of you, a force that cannot be slowed or stopped for it is of God; it is of Elohim; you are of Elohim; you are the sons and daughters of God. And to you, nothing is impossible.

19 "Now swirl the energy of your aura; swirl it faster and faster. At the bottom of every breath, before you inhale again, swirl your aura until you feel it inside of you at the core of your being, even your very soul essence.

20 "Now unify your breathing. Listen to the breath of the person to your right and to your left and be one with it. When they breathe in, you breathe in. When they breathe out, you breathe out.

21 "When you are at the bottom of your breath, do not breathe in again for several seconds as you spin your aura into your core and feel it radiating its power inside of you.

22 "Breathe in now in unison; as you breath out in unison, swirling your aura deeply inside at the bottom, forcefully say the Celestine word of power, "*Yizataz!*"

23 And so they all did; the men, the women and the children.

Immediately after they forcefully spoke *Yizataz* in unison, *Yeshua quickly spoke another sacred word of power; then another was spoken by Miriam, and then another by Cephas*. Then marvelous things began to occur.

24 A dense mist surrounded all the Children of Light. Where they stood was clear, but beyond them was only impenetrable mist.

25 Their own spirits spoke to them, giving them knowledge they had never learned, even so they all knew that the mist was a veil of illusion that none from the outside world would see anything at all upon the hill upon which they stood, except that which had always been there.

26 Then there was a sudden burst of yellow light in the middle of the circle that caused everyone to close their eyes for a moment because of the brightness. When they opened them again they were astounded to see several people standing before them that had not been there a moment ago.

27 After a few seconds, many of those in the circle began to discern who it was that had appeared and then their amazement was even greater.

28 For standing all around them both inside the circle and outside of it, were many of the Children of Light Yeshua had met in his travels over the many years.

Miriam Commands the Great Circle of Power of Celestine Lightening
Vivus 100:90-105

90 Looking once more into Miriam's eyes Yeshua said unto her. "Your time has begun my beloved. Command the Circles of Power."

91 Miriam kissed him one more time briefly, whispering "I love you," as she looked into his eyes. Continuing to hold her left arm about his waist, she turned to face the circle, saying, "Hold forth your wands, each and every one."

92 At her command all wands were drawn, some of wood, some of shell and some of crystal.

93 Then, still holding onto Yeshua by his waist with her left hand she drew her wand with her right and spun both of them around so they could pass in front of everyone in the circle.

94 "Look up into the heavens and point your wands skyward," she directed. And every wand quickly pointed to the sky.

95 Then she pointed her wand straight up and said unto them, "Unite

your auras as one. This is the Great Circle of Celestine Light.

96 "Send the aura that is one into the earth and call forth its power.

97 "Send the aura that is one into the heavens and call forth their power.

98 "Now as one let us say the *sacred word of Celestine summoning.*" With all wands raised to the sky, they spoke aloud, as one voice, the sacred Celestine word of summoning that cannot be written.

99 As the word escaped their lips for a third time brilliant beams of light shot forth from the tip of each wand, uniting as one and shooting straight up into the sky until it could be seen no more.

100 There was a tremendous rumbling upon the Earth and in the sky above like thunder from a thousand storms.

101 Still looking upward into the sky, they saw a sight such as no men had ever before seen. Though it was bright day, the sky was suddenly filled with brilliantly blazing shooting stars in a rainbow of hues, converging from points across the heavens into a single nexus of blazing white light far above them.

102 Miriam spoke to them again, saying, "Swirl the energy of the circle from east to west. Expand the light to fill the circle. Fill your aura with the light. Be one with the light."

103 Doing as she directed the circle was soon filled with a spinning vortex of white light that engulfed everyone. But each person, even the children, faithfully held their wands to the sky and kept their focus upon the light above.

104 Suddenly everyone's feet lifted off the ground and as a group the circle of Yeshua's closest disciples began to rise up into the sky. So intent was everyone in the circle upon their tasks that it seemed that not even one had noticed that their feet no longer stood upon the ground.

105 Higher and higher the Great Circle of Celestine Light rose up towards the convergence of the multicolored shooting stars, until suddenly they were among them and Miriam said, "Lower your wands and see where it is that you are, and who it is that you are among."

Examples of Words of Power
from the book "Destiny"

Excerpt from Chapter 5
Portals

Standing to Miriam's right she placed her hand upon my shoulder. "As you know, Lazarus has already traveled to other worlds, as has Salome," she added, glancing over and smiling at her long time companion sitting next to my wife Hannah.

"Today you will have the opportunity to visit several worlds very briefly so you can experience the different environments and become accustomed to some of the creatures that inhabit them.

"Some of you will travel to shadow worlds inhabited by beings of lesser light than any of the people or creatures of this Earth. Most of those creatures will hurt you if they can.

"Others will visit worlds that are as vibrant, beautiful and full of higher life as this one that we call home. Some of you will travel to places that have Alamars like you, but more primitive in their lifestyle. Others will have Alamars and similar races, but far more advanced in their civilization than those you have known.

"Do not be lulled into complacency by the beauty of the worlds or the similarities of the inhabitants to you. You will still be an unknown intruder and may be put to rapid execution if you are captured.

"Some of you will encounter more bizarre places where the inhabitants may be less or more advanced than you, but they will not be Alamars or in any way resemble Alamars. How will you react if you encounter a creature that for all appearances seems to be a giant bug, but is more intelligent than you and more advanced in its civilization then the cities you have known?

"Or perhaps you will encounter an enormous mosquito as large as you, that would like nothing better than to drain every drop of blood from your body.

"There will be dangers on any world you end up visiting. But you must come to know these worlds that connect to yours and the malevolent creatures that may someday come through portals where you will be the only defense to protect your world.

"To help you grow into this stewardship, it should be a goal of yours every day of your life to always be learning more, always gaining new knowledge about everything in existence.

"Knowledge is power. I exhort you to be knowledge sponges. Sometimes, standing alone, it is a greater power than your most potent Celestine gifts. But used in conjunction with abilities you have honed, knowledge allows you to better utilize your natural and blessed power. It insures a greater chance of success in any endeavor in direct proportion to the knowledge you have available to aid you."

Taking a couple of steps away from me, Miriam held her hands in the prayer position over her chest for a moment, bowed her head, then quickly looked up and thrust her palms still pressed together skyward. At their highest point she separated her hands, and lowered her extended arms sideways, while forcefully saying, "*Extavaz*."

Immediately we were encircled by numerous opaque, electric blue tunnels, with translucent spinning entrances, a little wider than the height of a man, leading outward from the courtyard and passing through anything they encountered from a wall to my house!

I quickly looked around and counted twelve in total. It was very weird looking at those that passed through my house. It was as if the rooms of my house, including my bedchamber, suddenly had large pipes running right through the middle of them.

As the the tunnels appeared everyone sitting at the tables stood up in shock, wonder, perhaps some fear of the unknown? There was quite a number of different looks on peoples faces.

Miriam encouraged everyone to walk around the courtyard and peer through the entrance of the various tunnels to see what they could perceive at the other end. There were soon many exclamations of amazement as everyone did as she bid and saw glimpses of the many worlds at the other end of the tunnels.

"These tunnels are all passageways to other worlds." Miriam explained as she walked among us while we peered through one tunnel entrance after another.

"Many are shadow worlds that occupy the same space as this Earth and the stars of these heavens. These worlds can not be seen by looking at the stars in the sky. Though they occupy the same space they are on a different level of energy. As thus, they are usually imperceptible. In most cases it is not an energy disharmonious to the energy of this world, it is merely different.

"Other portals lead to star worlds, which are places on the same physical plane as the Earth we live upon. If you had a ship that sailed the stars and could traverse the great distance between star worlds, you could travel on that ship and someday reach your destination. But star worlds can be reached in a much shorter time simply by traveling through a portal similar to one of these you now see in the courtyard."

Excerpt from Chapter 19

Angel of the Covenant

Lassoon looked intently at Miriam. "If it will bring back the Nagasas, release the Nartesians from your enchantment. If they are anything less than agreeable they will discover how frail their beautiful bodies really are when they can no longer control the mind of this former slave."

"As you wish." Miriam nodded in agreement to Lassoon's desire. She turned and faced the queen's box and the majority of the Nartesians still sitting placidly in the arena. She raised and crossed her arms in front of her and uttered the words releasing the Nartesians from their stupor and restoring them to their illusionary beauty as she drew her arms to her side. "*Kadaz! Frodka! Habalish!*"

The transformation of the Nartesian from doddering old people to ravishing beauties and ridiculously muscular men was startling, dramatic and nearly instantaneous. And they must have been fully aware of everything that had been taking place while they had been subdued and confined in old, mentally weak bodies, because the queen was instantly angry. She looked at Miriam with eyes burning with hatred. Given her illusion abilities I was expecting steam to start rising out of her ears any moment.

"You! You! You!" Leiaza screamed. I wasn't sure if she had returned with a defective limited vocabulary, or was just so upset she couldn't think of any other words at the moment.

"You dared to interfere with MY mind!" She yelled loudly, throwing her hands toward the ground and making the whole arena shake like a small earthquake.

Leiaza took a step forward and leaped over the rampart of the arena. She landed on her feet facing Miriam about four paces away. In the blink of an eye she materialized a large spear in her hand with a wicked looking, four-blade barbed metal point.

Without another word Leiaza stepped one foot forward and threw the spear with all of her might right toward Miriam. My sister just stood still, her hands clasped together and held low in front of her. She was as calm as a warm summer's morning, while I was in wide-eyed horror seeing the spear of doom streaking toward her heart. But before it found its mark it disintegrated into dust.

This only seemed to further incense Leiaza. She screamed in fury. "Palace guards to my side, war spears ready!"

Immediately at least two dozen burly warriors leaped over the rampart to join the queen facing Miriam. Each was armed with a even larger, more menacing spear than Leiaza's. The queen ordered them to form a half circle facing Miriam. She pointed at my sister.

"We are faced with a foe whose powers of the mind are as great as ours. But she is one and we are many. One spear she can turn to dust before it pierces her heart. I'm certain she will not fare as well with many. Kill her! Now!"

At her command all of the warriors launched their spears simultaneously. Miriam continued to stand in one place with her hands folded together down low. While the queen had been ranting, Miriam even looked up at the sky and around the arena for a moment as if she was bored by the whole affair.

Much to Leiaza's angry surprise the dozens of spears all flying together through the air toward Miriam met the same fate as the queens. Before they had traveled half the short distance they all became little glints of dirt and fell harmlessly to the ground.

The queen pointedly jabbed her finger in Miriam's direction. "You have talents vile one. But they will not avail you much longer. Everyone has a weakness. You cannot be strong in all areas of the mind. I promise you I will find your weakness shortly. Enjoy your final breaths of life. There shall not be many more!"

CONCLUSION

I hope reading Words of Power & Transformation has opened up a whole new world of possibilities and personal expansion for you. Whether you are a novice or an Adept, your potential is still much greater than you can imagine.

Despite the challenges of life that we all face, I encourage you to realize that you are different, in a very special sort of way, else you never would have been drawn to this book in the first place. Explore that difference. Expand upon it. Release yourself from the bonds of Mundania.

We live in an imperfect world; be in it but not of it. Through the cacophony of the demands of everyday life, allow yourself the space and time of reflection to soar to the heights of personal growth and magickal ability that call to you. Heed the quiet voice and gentle promptings of your inner Higher Self; it will always guide you true.

Namaste,

Embrosewyn

OTHER CAPTIVATING, THOUGHT-PROVOKING BOOKS BY EMBROSEWYN

CELESTINE LIGHT MAGICKAL SIGILS OF HEAVEN AND EARTH

What would happen if you could call upon the blessings of angels and amplify their miracles with the pure essence of spiritual magick?

Miracles manifest! That is the exciting reality that awaits you in *Celestine Light Magickal Sigils of Heaven and Earth.*

Calling upon the higher realm power of angels, through intentional summoning using specific magickal sigils and incantations, is considered to be the most powerful magick of all. But there is a magickal method even greater. When you combine calling upon a mighty angel with adding synergistic sigils and words of power, the amplification of the magickal energy can be astounding and the results that are manifested truly miraculous. This higher technique of magick is the essence of *Celestine Light Magickal Sigils of Heaven and Earth.*

This is the third book of the Magickal Celestine Light series and is an intermediate level reference book for students and practitioners of Celestine Light Magick. It contains a melding of the sigils and names of 99 of the 144 Angels found in *Angels of Miracles and Manifestation*, coupled with synergistic sigils and magickal incantations found within *Words of Power and Transformation.* To fully be able to implement the potent combination of angel magick and words of power magick revealed in this book, the practitioner should have previously read and have available as references the earlier two books in the series.

When magickal incantations and their sigils are evoked in conjunction with the summoning of an angel for a focused purpose, the magickal results are often exceptional. The potent combination of calling upon angels and amplifying your intent with words of power and sigils of spiritual magick creates an awesome, higher magickal energy that can manifest everyday miracles. Employing this potent form of magick can convert challenges into opportunities, powerfully counter all forms of negative magick, entities, phobias, fears and people, greatly enhance good fortune, and help change ordinary lives into the extraordinary.

ANGELS OF MIRACLES AND MANIFESTATION
144 Names, Sigils and Stewardships To Call
the Magickal Angels of Celestine Light

You are not alone. Whatever obstacle or challenge you face, whatever threat or adversary looms before you, whatever ability you seek to gain or mountain of life you want to conquer, divine angelic help is ready to intervene on your behalf. When the unlimited power of magickal angels stand with you, obstacles become opportunities, low times become springboards for better days, relationships blossom, illness becomes wellness, challenges become victories and miracles happen!

In *Angels of Miracles and Manifestation*, best-selling spiritual, magickal and paranormal author Embrosewyn Tazkuvel, reveals the secrets to summoning true magickal angels. And once called, how to use their awesome divine power to transform your compelling needs and desires into manifested reality.

Angel magick is the oldest, most powerful and least understood of all methods of magick. Ancient books of scripture from multiple religions tell of the marvelous power and miracles of angels. But the secrets of the true angel names, who they really are, their hierarchy, their stewardship responsibilities, their sigils, and how to successfully call them and have them work their divine magick for you, was lost to the world as a large part of it descended into the dark ages.

But a covenant was made by the Archangel Maeádael to the Adepts of Magick that as the people of the world evolved to a higher light the knowledge and power of angels would come again to the earth during the time of the Generation of Promise. That time is now. We are the Generation of Promise that has been foretold of for millennium. And all that was lost has been restored.

It doesn't matter what religion or path of enlightenment and empowerment that you travel: Wicca, Christianity, Pagan, Jewish, Buddhist, Occult, Muslim, Kabbalah, Vedic, something else or none at all. Nor does your preferred system of magick from Enochian, Thelemic, Gardnerian, Hermetic, to Tantric matter. Once you know the true names of the mighty angels, their unique sigils, and the simple but specific way to summon them, they will come and they will help you.

This revealing book of the ancient Celestine Light magick gives you immediate access to the divine powers of 14 Archangels, 136 Stewardship

Angels, and hundreds of Specialty Angels that serve beneath them. Whether you are a novice or a magickal Adept you will find that when angels are on your side you manifest results that you never imagined possible except in your dreams.

The angel magick of Celestine Light is simple and direct without a lot of ritual, which makes it easy even for the novice to be able to quickly use it and gain benefit. While there is a place and importance to ritual in other types of magickal conjuring it is not necessary with angels. They are supernatural beings of unlimited power and awareness whose stewardship includes responding quickly to people in need who call upon them. You do not need elaborate rituals to get their attention.

If you are ready to have magick come alive in your life; if you are ready for real-life practical results that bring wisdom, happiness, health, love and abundance; if you are ready to unveil your life's purpose and unleash your own great potential, obtain the treasure that is this book. Call upon the magickal angels and they will come. But be prepared. When you summon angels, the magick happens and it is transformative. Your life will improve in ways big and small. But it will never be the same.

Want to know more? Take a moment to click on the Look Inside tab in the upper left of this page to see the full extent of the marvels that await you inside this book!

AURAS
How To See, Feel & Know

***Auras: How to See, Feel & Know,* is like three books in one!**

1. It's an information packed, full color, complete training manual with 17 time tested exercises and 47 photos and illustrations to help you quickly be able to see Auras in vibrant color! It is the only full color book on auras available.

2. An entertaining read as Embrosewyn recalls his early childhood and high school experiences seeing auras, and the often humorous reactions by everyone from his mother to his friends when he told them what he saw.

3. Plus, a fascinating chapter on body language. Embrosewyn teaches in his workshops to not just rely on your interpretation of the aura alone, but to confirm it with another indicator such as body language.*Auras: How to See, Feel & Know*, goes in depth with thorough explanations and great pictures to show you all the common body language indicators used to confirm what someone's aura is showing you.

Auras includes:
- 17 dynamic eye exercises to help you rapidly begin to see the beautiful world of auras!
- 47 full color pictures and illustrations (in the Kindle or Full Color print edition).

Anyone with vision in both eyes can begin seeing vividly colored auras around any person with just 5 minutes of practice!

Learn how to:
- See the 7 layers of the aura using Embrosewyn's pioneering technique
- Understand the meaning of the patterns and shadows observed in the layers
- Train your eyes to instantly switch back and forth from aura to normal vision
- Understand the meaning and nuances of every color of the rainbow in an aura
- Use your aura as a shield against negative energy or people
- Power up your aura to have greater achievement in any endeavor

- Interpret body language to confirm observations of the aura
- Cut negative energy cords to disharmonious people
- Understand health conditions and ailments through the aura

The secret to aura sight is to retrain the focusing parts of your eyes to see things that have always been there, but you have never been able to see before. It's really not complicated. Anyone can do it using Embrosewyn's proven techniques and eye exercises. The author has been seeing brightly colored auras for over 60 years and teaching others to begin seeing auras within 5 minutes for the last 22 years. *Auras: How to See, Feel & Know*, includes all the power techniques, tools and Full Color eye exercises from his popular workshops.

For those who already have experience seeing auras, the deeper auric layers and subtle auric nuances and the special ways to focus your eyes to see them, are explained in detail, with Full Color pictures and illustrations to show you how the deeper layers and auric aberrations appear. It is also a complete training manual to help you quickly be able to see Auras in vibrant color. It includes 17 eye exercises and dozens of Full Color pictures, enabling anyone with vision in both eyes to begin seeing vividly colored auras around any person. The secret is in retraining the focusing parts of your eyes to see things that have always been there, but you have never been able to see before. *Auras: How to See, Feel & Know*, includes all the power techniques, tools and Full Color eye exercises from Embrosewyn's popular workshops.

Additionally, there is a fascinating chapter on body language. Embrosewyn teaches in his workshops to not just rely on your interpretation of the aura alone, but to confirm it with another indicator such as body language. *Auras: How to See, Feel & Know* goes in depth with thorough explanations and great pictures to show you all the common body language indicators used to confirm what someone's aura is showing you.

For those who already have experience seeing auras, the deeper auric layers and subtle auric nuances and the special ways to focus your eyes to see them, are explained in detail, with accompanying Full Color pictures to show you how the deeper layers and auric aberrations appear.

SOUL MATE AURAS
How To Find Your Soul Mate & "Happily Ever After"

The romantic dream of finding your Soul Mate, the person with whom you resonate on every level of your being, is more than a wishful notion. It is a deeply embedded, primal desire that persists on some level despite what may have been years of quiet, inner frustration and included relationships that while fulfilling on some levels, still fell short of the completeness of a Soul Mate.

Once found, your relationship with your Soul Mate can almost seem like a dream at times. It will be all you expected and probably much more. Having never previously had a relationship that resonated in harmony and expansiveness on every level of your being, you will have had nothing to prepare you for its wonder. Having never stood atop a mountain that tall with an expansiveness so exhilarating, once experienced, a committed relationship with your Soul Mate will give you a bliss and fulfillment such as you probably only imagined in fairy tales.

But how to find your Soul Mate? That is the million dollar question. The vast majority of people believe finding your Soul Mate is like a magnetic attraction, it will somehow just happen; in some manner you'll just be inevitably drawn to each other. The harsh reality is, 99% of people realize by their old age that it never happened. Or, if it did occur they didn't recognize their Soul Mate at the time, because they were looking for a different ideal.

Soul Mate Auras: How To Find Your Soul Mate & Happily Ever After gives you the master keys to unlock the passageway to discovering your Soul Mate using the certainty of your auric connections. Every person has a unique aura and auric field generated by their seven energy centers and their vitality. Find the person that you resonate strongly with on all seven energy centers and you'll find your Soul Mate!

Everyone can sense and see auras. In *Soul Mate Auras* full color eye and energy exercises will help you learn how to see and feel auras and how to use that ability to identify where in the great big world your Soul Mate is living. Once you are physically in the presence of your prospective Soul Mate, you will know how to use your aura to energetically confirm that they are the one. The same methods can be used to discover multiple people that are Twin Flames with you; not quite seven auric connection Soul Mates, but still deep and expansive connections to you on five to six energy centers.

Soul Mate Auras also includes an in-depth procedure to determine if someone is a Twin Flame or Soul Mate, not by using your aura, but by honestly and rationally evaluating your connections on all seven of your energy centers. This is an invaluable tool for anyone contemplating marriage or entering a long-term committed relationship. It also serves as a useful second opinion confirmation for anyone that has used their aura to find their Soul Mate.

To help inspire and motivate you to create your own "happily ever after," *Soul Mate Auras* is richly accentuated with dozens of full color photos of loving couples along with profound quotes from famous to anonymous people about the wonder of Soul Mates.

Treat yourself to the reality of finding your Soul Mate or confirming the one that you have already found! Scroll to the upper left of the page and click on Look Inside to find out more about what's inside this book!

Secret Earth Series

INCEPTION
BOOK 1

Could it be possible that there is a man alive on the Earth today that has been here for two thousand years? How has he lived so long? And why? What secrets does he know? Can his knowledge save the Earth or is it doomed?

Continuing the epic historical saga begun in the *Oracles of Celestine Light*, but written as a novel rather than a chronicle, *Inception* unveils the life and adventures of Lazarus of Bethany and his powerful and mysterious sister Miriam of Magdala.

The first book of the Secret Earth series, *Inception*, reveals the hidden beginnings of the strange, secret life of Lazarus. From his comfortable position as the master of caravans to Egypt he is swept into a web of intrigue involving his enigmatic sister Miriam and a myriad of challenging dangers that never seem to end and spans both space and time.

Some say Miriam is an angel, while others are vehement that she is a witch. Lazarus learns the improbable truth about his sister, and along with twenty-three other courageous men and women, is endowed with the secrets of immortality. But he learns that living the secrets is not as easy as knowing them. And living them comes at a price; one that needs to be paid in unwavering courage, stained with blood, built with toil, and endured with millenniums of sacrifice, defending the Earth from all the horrors that might have been. *Inception* is just the beginning of their odyssey.

DESTINY
BOOK 2

In preparation, before beginning their training as immortal Guardians of the Earth, Lazarus of Bethany and his wife Hannah were asked to go on a short visit to a world in another dimension. "Just to look around a bit and get a feel for the differences," Lazarus's mysterious sister, Miriam of Magdala assured them.

She neglected to mention the ravenous monstrous birds, the ferocious fire-breathing dragons, the impossibly perfect people with sinister ulterior motives, and the fact that they would end up being naked almost all the time! And that was just the beginning of the challenges!

UNLEASH YOUR PSYCHIC POWERS

A Comprehensive 400 Page Guidebook

Unleash Your Psychic Powers is an entertaining, enlightening and educational resource for all levels of practitioners in the psychic, magickal and paranormal arts. It includes easy-to-follow, step-by-step instructions on how you can develop and enhance the full potential of dynamic psychic, magickal and paranormal powers in your own life.

Whether You Are A Novice Or An Adept

You will find valuable insight and guidance, based upon Embrosewyn's six decades of experience discovering and developing psychic and paranormal talents and unleashing the power of the magickal arts.

Twenty Psychic And Paranormal Abilities Are Explored

Including well known abilities such as Clairvoyance, Telekinesis, Telepathy, Lucid Dreaming, Precognition, Astral Projection and Faith Healing, plus, more obscure talents such as Channeling, Dowsing, and Automatic Handwriting.

In addition to helping you develop and master the psychic abilities that call to you, each of the twenty powers described are spiced with fascinating personal stories from the lives of Embrosewyn and others, to help you understand some of the real world consequences and benefits of using these formidable magickal and psychic talents. Paranormal abilities have saved Embrosewyn's life and the lives of his family members on multiple occasions. Learning to fully develop your own psychic and paranormal abilities may come in just as handy one day.

For anyone that is an active spirit medium, or uses any psychic abilities involving other-worldly beings, such as divination, channeling, or ghost hunting, the chapter on Psychic Self-defense is an extensive must read, covering low, medium and high risk threats, including everything from negative vortexes, to entities, energy vampires, ghosts, aliens and demons. Exorcism, and how to protect both people and property from unseen forces is also completely explained.

Filled with pictures and vivid descriptions of how you can bring forth and develop your own transcendental supernatural gifts, *Unleash Your Psychic Powers* should be in the library of every serious student of the psychic, magickal, paranormal and supernatural.

Everyone has psychic and paranormal abilities. It is your birthright! You were born with them!

Within this book you'll learn how to unlock and unleash your astounding supernatural potential and the amazing things you can do with your powers once they are free!

PSYCHIC SELF DEFENSE

A Complete Guide to Protecting Yourself Against Psychic & Paranormal Attack (and just plain irksome people)

Felt a negative energy come over you for no apparent reason when you are near someone or around certain places? Had a curse hurled at you? Spooked by a ghost in a building? Imperiled by demonic forces? Being drained and discombobulated by an energy vampire? Or, do you encounter more mundane but still disruptive negative energies like an over demanding boss, the local bully, hurtful gossip, a physically or mentally abusive spouse, or life in a dangerous neighborhood threatened by thieves and violence? Whatever your source of negative energy, danger or threat, you'll find effective, proven, psychic and magickal countermeasures within this book.

Psychic Self Defense draws upon Embrosewyn's six decades of personal experience using psychic abilities and magickal defenses to thwart, counter and send back to sender, any and all hostile paranormal threats. Everything from unsupportive and dismissive family and friends, to ghosts, demons and exorcisms. The same practical and easy to learn Magickal techniques can be mastered by anyone serious enough to give it some time and practice, and can aid you immensely with a host of material world challenges as well.

17 psychic and paranormal threats are covered with exact, effective counter measures, including many real life examples from Embrosewyn's comprehensive personal experiences with the paranormal, devising what works and what doesn't from hard won trial and error.

Whether you are a medium needing to keep foul spirits away, or simply someone desiring to know that you, your family and property are safe and protected, you will find the means to insure peace and security with the proven methods outlined in *Psychic Self Defense*

You will learn how to:
- Create your own Magick spells tailored to your particular situation and need
- Call upon specific angels to aid you
- Create Crystal Energy Shields
- Protect yourself when in a channeling or spirit medium trance
- Use your Aura to create ASP's (Auric Shields of Power)

- Empower Wards for protection against specific threats
- Recognize and counter Energy Vampires
- Cleanse a home of negative energy
- Cut negative energy cords to disharmonious people
- Counter Black Magick
- Detect alien presence
- Banish malicious entities or demons

Though dealing with numerous and sometimes dangerous other-worldly and material world threats, the entire approach of this book is from a position of personal empowerment, no fear, and divine white light. Whether you are religious or an atheist, an experienced practitioner of the psychic and magickal arts or a neophyte, someone living in a haunted house or just an employee wanting to have a nicer boss, there will be hundreds of ways you can use the information in this book to help you in your life. And you will learn to do it in ways that are uplifting and empowering, producing results that are peaceful, safe and harmonious.

Psychic Self Defense is also available as an AUDIO BOOK.

22 STEPS TO THE LIGHT OF YOUR SOUL

A Treasured Book That Will Help You Unleash The Greatness Within

What would it be like if you could reach through space and time to query the accumulated wisdom of the ages and get an answer? 22 Steps to the Light of Your Soul, reveals such treasured insights, eloquently expounding upon the foundational principles of 22 timeless subjects of universal interest and appeal, to help each reader grow and expand into their fullest potential.

In a thought-provoking, poetic writing style, answers to questions we all ponder upon, such as love, happiness, success and friendship, are explored and illuminated in short, concise chapters, perfect for a thought to ponder through the day or contemplate as your eyes close for sleep.

Each paragraph tells a story and virtually every sentence could stand alone as an inspiring quote on your wall.

These are the 22 steps of the Light of Your Soul
Step 1: The Purpose of Life
Step 2: Balance
Step 3: Character
Step 4: Habits
Step 5: Friendship
Step 6: True Love
Step 7: Marriage
Step 8: Children
Step 9: Happiness
Step 10: Play & Relaxation
Step 11: Health
Step 12: Success
Step 13: Knowledge
Step 14: Passion & Serenity
Step 15: Imagination & Vision
Step 16: Creativity & Art
Step 17: Adversity
Step 18: Respect
Step 19: Freedom & Responsibility
Step 20: Stewardship

Step 21: Faith
Step 22: Love Yourself - the Alpha and the Omega

ALSO AVAILABLE AS AN AUDIO BOOK! You can listen as you commute to work or travel on vacation, or even listen and read together!

LOVE YOURSELF
The Secret Key to Transforming Your Life

Loving yourself is all about energy

As humans we devote a great deal of our energy through our time, thoughts and emotions to love. We read about it, watch movies and shows about it, dream about it, hope for it to bless our lives, feel like something critically important is lacking when it doesn't, and at the very least keep a sharp eye out for it when its missing.

Too often we look to someone else to fulfill our love and crash and burn when relationships end, or fail to live up to our fantasies of what we thought they should be. When we seek love from another person or source greater than the love we give to ourselves, we set ourselves up to an inevitable hard landing when the other person or source ceases to provide the level of fulfillment we desire.

Loving yourself is a precious gift from you to you. It is an incredibly powerful energy that not only enhances your ability to give love more fully to others, it also creates a positive energy of expanding reverberation that brings more love, friendship and appreciation to you from all directions. It is the inner light that illuminates your life empowering you to create the kind of life you desire and dream.

The relationship you have with yourself is the most important one in your life. Happiness will forever be fleeting if you do not have peace, respect and love for yourself. It's not selfish. It's not vain. It is in fact the key to transforming your life. Inward reflection and appreciation will open up clearer channels to the divine. Relationships with everyone will be enhanced as your relationship with yourself expands and is uplifted.

All other relationships are only mirrors of the one you have within. As you love yourself, are kind to yourself, respect yourself, so too will you be able to give those and so many other good qualities to others in equal measure to that which you give to yourself.

This is a short, but very sweet book to help you discover your inner glow of love. Within its covers are two great keys you will find no other place. These two keys will proactively bring you to the serenity of self-love regardless of whether you are currently near or far from that place of peace.

Are you familiar with the infinity symbol? It looks pretty much like the number 8 turned on its side. As love for yourself should be now and forever, in the last chapter you will find 88 reasons why loving yourself is vitally important to your joy, personal growth and expansion, and the happiness of everyone whose lives you touch. Most people have never considered that there could be a list that long just about loving yourself! But with each short phrase you read your mind begins to understand to a greater depth how important loving yourself is for all aspects of your life and relationships. As your mind understands your life follows.

This book leaves you with a special gift Inside you'll find two short, but very valuable multimedia flash presentations. One is entitled "Forgive Yourself". The other is "Love Yourself" These are not normal flash presentations. They are self-hypnosis, positive affirmations that will rapidly help you achieve greater self-love and more fulfilling love-filled realities in your life. As soft repetitive music plays in the background, images reinforcing the theme will flash by on your screen about three per second, accompanied by short phrases superimposed on a portion of the image. In a quick 7-10 minute session, sitting at home in front of your computer, you will find the flash presentations buoy and motivate you. Repeat them twice a day for several days and you will find they are transformative.

Special Bonus: *Love Yourself* is ALSO AVAILABLE AS AN AUDIO BOOK! This allows you to listen and read at the same time!

ORACLES OF CELESTINE LIGHT
COMPLETE TRILOGY OF GENESIS, NEXUS & VIVUS

Once in a lifetime comes a book that can dramatically change your life for the better - forever. This is it!

WHAT WAS LOST...HAS BEEN FOUND

This is the complete 808 page trilogy of the Celestine books of Light: Genesis, Nexus and Vivus.

The controversial *Oracles of Celestine Light*, is a portal in time to the days of Yeshua of Nazareth, over 2000 years ago, revealed in fulfilling detail to the world by the reclusive Embrosewyn Tazkuvel. It includes 155 chapters of sacred wisdom, miracles and mysteries revealing life-changing knowledge about health, longevity, happiness and spiritual expansion that reverberates into your life today.

Learn the startling, never before understood truth:

About aliens, other dimensions, Atlantis, Adam & Eve, the Garden of Eden, Noah and the ark, giants, the empowerment of women, dreams, angels, Yeshua of Nazareth (Jesus), his crucifixion & resurrection, his wife Miriam of Magdala (Mary Magdala), Yudas Iscariot (Judas), the afterlife, reincarnation, energy vortexes, witches, magic, miracles, paranormal abilities, and you!

The **Or**acles of Celestine Light turns accepted religious history and traditional teachings on their head. But page by page, it makes more sense than anything you've ever read and shares simple yet profound truths to make your life better today and help you to understand and unleash your miraculous potential.

The *Oracles of Celestine Light* explains who you are, why you are here, and your divine destiny. It is a must-read for anyone interested in spirituality, personal growth and thought-provoking answers to the unknown.

"You are a child of God, a Child of Light, literally a priceless son or daughter of divinity. Even through the fog of mortal upheavals and the tumults and tribulations, always remember you are still a child of God and shall inherit joy and kingdoms beyond measure, as you remain true to your light." Genesis 11:99

Psychic Awakening Series
CLAIRVOYANCE

Would it be helpful if you could gain hidden knowledge about a person, place, thing, event, or concept, not by any of your five physical senses, but with visions and "knowing?"

Are you ready to supercharge your intuition? *Clairvoyance* takes you on a quest of self-discovery and personal empowerment, helping you unlock this potent ESP ability in your life. It includes riveting stories from Embrosewyn's six decades of psychic and paranormal adventures, plus fascinating accounts of others as they discovered and cultivated their supernatural abilities.

Clearly written, step-by-step practice exercises will help you to expand and benefit from your own psychic and clairvoyant abilities. This can make a HUGE improvement in your relationships, career and creativity. As Embrosewyn has proven from over twenty years helping thousands of students to find and develop their psychic and paranormal abilities, EVERYONE, has one or more supernatural gifts. *Clairvoyance* will help you discover and unleash yours!

If you are interested in helping yourself to achieve more happiness, better health, greater knowledge, increased wealth and a deeper spirituality, unlocking your power of clairvoyance can be the key. Hidden knowledge revealed becomes paths unseen unveiled.

Unleashing your psychic gifts does more than just give you advantage in life challenges. It is a safe, ethical, even spiritual and essential part of you that makes you whole, once you accept that you have these special psychic abilities and begin to use them.

TELEKINESIS

Easy, comprehensive guide for anyone wanting to develop the supernatural ability of Telekinesis

Telekinesis, also known as psychokinesis, is the ability to move or influence the properties of objects without physical contact. Typically it is ascribed as a power of the mind. But as Embrosewyn explains, based upon his sixty years of personal experience, the actual physical force that moves and influences objects emanates from a person's auric field. It initiates with a mental thought, but the secret to the power is in your aura!

Telekinesis is the second book in the Psychic Awakening series by popular paranormal writer Embrosewyn Tazkuvel. The series was specifically created to offer short, inexpensive, information filled handbooks to help you quickly learn and develop specific psychic and paranormal abilities.

Clearly written, *Telekinesis* is filled with step-by-step practice exercises and training techniques proven to help you unlock this formidable paranormal ability. Spiced with riveting accounts of real-life psychic experiences and paranormal adventures, you'll be entertained while you learn. But along the way you will begin to unleash the potent power of Telekinesis in your own life!

As Embrosewyn has proven from over twenty years helping thousands of students to find and develop their psychic and paranormal abilities. EVERYONE, has one or more supernatural gifts. Is Telekinesis one of yours? Perhaps it's time to find out.

DREAMS

Awaken in the world of your sleep

In *Dreams*, the third book of the Psychic awakening series, renowned psychic/paranormal practitioner Embrosewyn Tazkuvel reveals some of his personal experiences with the transformational effect of dreams, while sharing time-tested techniques and insights that will help you unlock the power of your own night travels.

Lucid Dreaming

An expanded section on Lucid Dreaming gives you proven methods to induce and develop your innate ability to control your dreams. It explores the astonishing hidden world of your dream state that can reveal higher knowledge, greatly boost your creativity, improve your memory, and help you solve vexing problems of everyday life that previously seemed to have no solution.

Nine Types of Dreams

Detailing the nine types of dreams will help you to understand which dreams are irrelevant and which you should pay close attention to, especially when they reoccur. You'll gain insight into how to interpret the various types of dreams to understand which are warnings and which are gems of inspiration that can change your life from the moment you awaken and begin to act upon that which you dreamed.

Become the master of your dreams

Sleeping and dreaming are a part of your daily life that cumulatively accounts for dozens of years of your total life. It is a valuable time of far more than just rest. Become the master of your dreams and your entire life can become more than you ever imagined possible. Your dreams are the secret key to your future.

Additional Services Offered by Embrosewyn

I am honored to be able to be of further service to you by offering multiple paranormal abilities for your enlightenment and life assistance. On a limited basis as my time allows I can:

- discover your Soul Name and the meaning and powers of the sounds

- custom craft and imbue enchantments upon a piece of your jewelry for a wide beneficial range of purposes

- discover the name of your Guardian Angel

- have an in-depth psychic consultation and Insight Card reading with you via a Skype video call.

My wife Sumara can also create a beautiful piece of collage art on 20"x30" internally framed canvas, representing all of the meanings and powers of the sounds of your Soul Name.

If you are interested in learning more about any of these additional services please visit my website: *www.embrosewyn.com* and click on the link at the top for SERVICES.

If you would like to purchase enchanted jewelry or gemstones for specific purposes such as love, health, good fortune, or psychic protection please visit my website: *www.magickalgems.com.*

For great info on a wide variety of psychic, paranormal and magick subjects, please visit my YouTube Channel, *Esoteric Mystery School with*

Embrosewyn Tazkuvel.

NOTES